Bourbon

Creme

Killer

Book Nine in

The INNcredibly Sweet Series

By

Summer Prescott

Author's note: I'd love to hear your thoughts on my books, the storylines, and anything else that you'd like to comment on—reader feedback is very important to me. My contact information, along with some other helpful links, is listed below. If you'd like to be on my list of "folks to contact" with updates, release and sales notifications, etc.… just shoot me an email and let me know. Thanks for reading!

Also…

… if you're looking for more great reads, I am proud to announce that Summer Prescott Books publishes a popular series by new cozy author Patti Benning. Check out my book catalog

http://summerprescottbooks.com/book-catalog/ for her delicious stories.

Contact Info for Summer Prescott:

Twitter: @summerprescott1

Blog and Book Catalog:
http://summerprescottbooks.com

Email: summer.prescott.cozies@gmail.com

Please note: If you receive any correspondence from addresses other than those listed here, it is not from me, even if it claims to be.

And... look me up on Facebook—let's be friends!

If you're an author and are interested in publishing with Summer Prescott Books, please send me an email and I'll send you submission guidelines.

BOURBON CREME

KILLER

Book Nine in The INNcredibly Sweet Series

TABLE OF CONTENTS

CHAPTER ONE

Melissa Gladstone-Beckett eyed the untouched vegan lemon chiffon cupcake sitting in front of her best friend, flame-haired, gypsy-souled Echo Willis, with a concerned frown.

"You're not eating, darlin," she said softly, her southern accent conspicuous. Missy always seemed to slip back into her Louisiana drawl whenever she was worried about something.

"I feel icky," Echo groaned, leaning her head on her hand.

The forty-something free spirit had very recently found out that she was three months pregnant. Her fiancé was thrilled, but she was terrified. A severe case of morning sickness wasn't helping matters, so her southern friend was constantly trying to feed her and keep her hydrated.

"Well, cupcakes probably aren't what you need anyway," Missy mused. "Can I make you some soup or pasta or something?"

Echo turned green at the mere thought of food, and shook her head.

"I want coffee."

"I know you do, sweetie, but the doctor said that you need to cut down…" she began.

"Yeah, yeah," Echo waved her off weakly. "I swear that doctor hates me. No coffee, no wine, and I'm supposed to take in more calcium and protein, yuck."

Missy chuckled. "Oh come on, it's not as bad as all that. He didn't say NO coffee or wine, he just said that you had to closely watch your intake. How about some rice with banana?"

"If I say yes, will you stop bugging me about food?" her friend gave her a faint grin.

"For now," she chuckled, then kissed Echo on the top of the head and went to the kitchen to mash some bananas.

While Missy was in the kitchen of Cupcakes in Paradise, the cozy little shop that she owned and operated, Echo's fiancé, Phillip "Kel" Kellerman came in and sat down next to his beloved at their favorite bistro table in the eating area.

"Hey Kel," Missy greeted him, setting down Echo's breakfast in front of her.

"Good morning, lovely lady. I see that someone has finally succeeded in getting this delicate creature to eat," he lovingly stroked the back of Echo's hand.

"Well, not yet, but I'm trying. How's life with you?" Missy asked, gathering a mug of coffee and a Bourbon Creme cupcake and setting them down in front of him.

Kel was a local, world-renowned artist in his early sixties who thought that the sun rose and set in Echo's eyes and smile. He'd loved her from the moment he'd met her, and now he was delighted at the prospect of marrying her and raising their baby together.

"Never better. I have a show in Atlanta next week, so I'm hoping that you'll keep an eye on my bride-to-be while I'm gone," he announced, taking a huge bite of cupcake.

"I'm not a toddler, I don't need a babysitter," Echo folded her arms crossly.

"You sound like one at the moment," Missy grinned. "Now quit pouting and eat your breakfast," she teased.

Echo raised an eyebrow then stuck out her tongue, barely suppressing a grin, but she picked up her spoon and began eating the mush in front of her.

"I don't know why, it's just going to come up later anyway," she muttered, grimacing.

"Are you going to eat that cupcake then?" her fiancé asked, eyeing the treat and putting his hands up defensively when he saw her glare.

"Okay, okay, sorry. I just didn't want it to go to waste."

Missy giggled at their antics, her heart warm with love for both of them.

"So… in light of recent events," she said casually, referring to the news that Echo was pregnant. "Have you two thought about maybe setting a wedding date?"

"Well, my dear lady, as you well know, I would marry this beautiful lass at the drop of a hat, but she's been quite adept at dragging her feet thus far," Kel gazed at his beloved affectionately over the top of his stylish wire-rimmed glasses.

Echo put her spoon down and wound her fingers through Kel's.

"I've been thinking about that," she began, blushing. "I think that we should…"

Missy and Kel both leaned forward, listening intently.

"I think we should get married before the baby comes," she gazed up at her adoring fiancé, touched by the sweet surprise that she saw in his eyes.

Missy clapped her hands with glee.

"Oh honey, that's wonderful," she practically bounced out of her chair with delight. "We've got to start planning. We'll have the reception at the inn of course," she said, referring to the beachside bed and breakfast that she owned with her dashing and clever husband, Detective Chas Beckett. The Beach House was right next door to her cupcake shop and was seamlessly run by Maggie, the innkeeper. It would be a perfect location for a wedding reception.

Echo shook her head and interrupted her friend.

"No, we don't need to plan, it's not going to be that involved. We'll just go to the courthouse with whoever can be there, and we don't need a reception. I can't drink anyway," she smiled.

Kel was clearly thunderstruck.

"If that's okay with you," she said softly.

"My beloved, you have made all of my dreams come true in this moment," he brought her hand to his lips. "We shall do whatever you think is best, and the sooner the better."

Missy blinked at her friend, excited that she'd finally made up her mind about when to get married, but more than a bit disappointed that she wouldn't be able to throw the reception of the century for her best friend's wedding.

Echo grinned at Kel, seeming relieved.

"Well, Grayson and Sarah are going to be coming down here to get married in two months, and I don't want to steal any of their thunder, so I'd like for it to happen before then. How about next week? That way Missy and I will have time to shop for new dresses."

Grayson Myers, whom Missy and Chas had met while living in LaChance, Louisiana, was like a son to them. When the couple moved to Florida from Louisiana, Missy had given her cupcake shop in LaChance to the talented young man as a present for his graduation from art school. His artistry with cupcakes was legendary, and he'd improved on what Missy had taught him about cupcakes.

"Next week," Kel beamed. "Next week this amazing woman will be my bride. Works for me."

He glanced over at Missy who nodded enthusiastically, her eyes shining.

"I'm so happy for you two," she grinned, her happiness spilling over onto her cheeks as she squeezed their hands across the table.

"I'm off then," Kel replied, standing to go and grabbing Echo's cupcake. "I have to find a tuxedo."

"Oh Kel, a tux? To a courthouse wedding?" Echo protested, reaching to snatch the cupcake from him and missing.

"Indeed, my love. I'm only getting married once, and it certainly won't be in a suit," he grinned, holding the cupcake aloft and heading for the door.

"That means my dress will be expensive," she taunted.

"My credit card is at your service, ma'am," he shot back, stuffing the cupcake in his mouth on his way out the door.

"That man is just like a teenager," Missy giggled, watching him go.

"So it seems," Echo remarked, gazing after him thoughtfully.

CHAPTER TWO

Phillip "Kel" Kellerman walked with an extra bounce in his step these days. In just over a week, he'd finally be marrying the woman of his dreams, who was also going to be the mother of his child. He'd never seriously considered fatherhood, but now the prospect of it filled him with joy. It was a feeling unlike any other he'd ever experienced. A proud, protective male instinct rose up within him every time he saw his glowing fiancée, and he was on top of the world, making sure her every need and want was fulfilled. His work had been inspired and his productivity had gone through the roof. The artist couldn't wait to take his new bride to Paris for their honeymoon and show her off to all of his friends in the French art scene, as well as spending some quality romantic time together.

Kel was checking his hair in the hall mirror one last time before heading out to his studio when the doorbell rang. He wasn't expecting any deliveries, and hadn't made any appointments with clients. Perplexed, he opened the front door and saw a handsome blue-eyed youth, whose floppy blond hair covered one eye. The teenaged boy was lean, almost hungry-looking, and seemed

19

strangely familiar, but Kel couldn't fathom where he might know him from. Pizza delivery maybe?

"Hello. What can I do for you, young man?" he asked, itching to get to his studio, but in good spirits.

"Umm… hi," the boy's eyes darted back and forth, and he was clearly nervous as he brushed his hair out of his eyes, causing Kel to look at him even more closely. There was something about those eyes. "Are you… uh… Phil Kellerman?" he asked, blushing furiously.

Kel chuckled. "No one ever calls me that, dear boy, but yes, I am he. What can I do for you?"

"Well, I… uh… I mean… can I come in and talk to you for a minute?" the lad asked, not quite meeting Kel's eyes.

The artist weighed his options. He didn't typically invite strangers into his home, but clearly the boy was no threat to him, and he figured that the sooner the boy asked for whatever it was that he wanted, the sooner he'd be on his way to the studio, so he opened the door wide and gestured for him to enter.

"Thanks," the blue-eyed waif said softly, ducking his head as he went by.

Kel sunk into his favorite club chair and gestured to the couch. The boy sat obediently, looking very uncomfortable and obviously in awe of his surroundings.

"You're an artist," he observed, wide-eyed.

"Indeed. Now what is it that brought you to my door, young man?" Kel asked pleasantly.

"This is a little embarrassing, sir," he murmured.

"No worries, this is a judgment-free zone. Out with it," the artist encouraged.

"My name is Scott. Scott Hammond," the youth began, picking at a hangnail rather than looking at Kel.

The name rang a bell somewhere in the back of the older man's mind, but again, he couldn't determine why.

"Nice to meet you, Scott."

"Thank you, sir. So, the reason that I'm here is that… well, my mom is missing, and…" he began.

"Good heavens," Kel exclaimed, interrupting. "Have you called the police?" He now figured that the boy must look familiar because he lived nearby.

"Uh… no. I can't," he looked helpless and embarrassed all at once.

"Why not?"

"Because I think she might be in danger and I think that it might be worse if I go to the cops… uh, police."

"Are you in danger?" Kel leaned forward, frowning.

"I don't know. I don't think so, at least, not for now, while I'm here in Florida," Scott sighed.

"Where else would you be?" the artist was confused. "Aren't you from here?"

"No sir, I'm from Illinois."

"Well, you're a long way from home," he observed, growing more befuddled by the second. "Why don't you start at the beginning and tell me what you're doing here, and what led to you appearing on my doorstep."

"Okay," Scott nodded, taking a breath. Kel got up and got him a glass of water. "Thanks," he said, drinking deeply. "So, my mom was dating this guy for a while, and things seemed fine, but after her car broke down and she got it fixed, they started arguing a lot. I don't know what they were arguing about, but she always seemed pretty upset afterwards."

"So, you think that her boyfriend might have had something to do with her disappearance?" Kel interrupted.

"I think it's possible. I mean, she'd never just stay gone without talking to me about it, or at least calling or texting or something," Scott shrugged, looking scared.

Kel chose his next words carefully. "Forgive me if I sound callous, because that's certainly not my intention, but what does the disappearance of a woman from Illinois have to do with me? How did you even know my name? Are you a budding artist? And how did you get here?"

Scott took another deep breath and set down his glass.

"I do enjoy art... a lot. I paint and sculpt and make things out of other people's trash, but that's not how I found you," the color rose in his cheeks again.

"I was really worried about my mom, so I looked through her desk, I even used my pocketknife to unlock the locked drawers, and I found a box. It was wooden and really pretty. I felt bad because when I jimmied the lock, it broke off a chunk of wood, but I figured she'd understand," the youth rambled.

"So anyway, in the box was a bundle of letters and they were all from the same person... you."

"Letters?" Kel was baffled.

"Well, more like personal notes. They didn't go through the mail or anything," Scott squirmed a bit.

"Scott… who is your mother?"

"Jeanette, Jeanette Hammond," he said, looking the man squarely in the eye.

Suddenly Kel couldn't breathe, and had to take a moment to gather his wits.

"I haven't heard that name in…" he began, staring into the distance.

"About fifteen years?" the youth asked.

Kel's eyes went wide and refocused on his visitor. "Do you… are you saying… ?"

"Yes, sir," Scott nodded. "I went through the letters and looked at the dates. The last one was dated seven months before my birthday. You're… my father."

"Jeanette was…" Kel paled at the realization that his former girlfriend had known she was pregnant when she had moved away forever.

He stared at the youth, blinking and now realized why the boy's eyes looked so familiar… it was like looking into a mirror, and the floppy blond hair looked much like Kel's had at the same age.

"I don't know what to say," he whispered hoarsely.

"Well, sir, the way that I see it, we can worry about all of that later. I had enough money to take a bus to Georgia, and I hitchhiked the rest of the way because I need help finding my mom," Scott replied earnestly, his blush reaching the tips of his ears.

"How did you find me?" Kel asked, in a daze.

"I did an internet search and found a name that matched, in the town that was on Mom's birth certificate. It seemed to be pretty obvious," the determined youth shrugged.

Kel nodded, his heart thumping in his chest. "Okay, then."

CHAPTER THREE

Echo Willis was the proud owner of a handmade candle shop downtown, and the adjoining bookstore that had been willed to her when its owner passed away. She'd made an open archway between the two shops and had hired a spunky young woman named Joyce Rutledge to run the bookstore, while she presided over the candle side. This morning, the book store had been abuzz, but the candle shop had been relatively quiet, for which she was thankful. She hadn't planned on getting pregnant, and had had no idea of how tired she'd be all the time. The little one that she carried within her was only the size of a peanut, but its presence weighed on her mightily.

"Whew! Lord, Miss Echo," Joyce came over to the candle counter during a lull in the action, fanning herself with her hands. "I thought that line was never going to wind down."

Echo leaned wearily against the counter.

"I'm so thankful that you're here to help me handle this," she smiled weakly.

Joyce pursed her lips and raised an eyebrow, assessing her boss.

"I know that you and I come from different worlds on this, ma'am, but that baby you've got is just crying out for some real food. That vegan stuff is fine for adults, but that child's got bones and organs that need to develop and grow. You need to eat some meat, girl," she admonished. "You just say the word and I'll bring in some hearty helpings of soul food. My cornbread and barbecued brisket is just what you need, mark my words."

Echo blinked at her assistant, turned a pale shade of green and bolted for the bathroom.

"Or not," Joyce remarked dryly. "Take your time, Miss Echo, I got this," she called after her boss, shaking her head. "Maybe if you ate some macaroni with real cheese instead of all those vegetables, your food would stay down better," she muttered, picking up a vanilla-cupcake-scented candle and sniffing it.

"Hey, Mr. Kel," Joyce greeted Echo's fiancé, when the chimes above the door tinkled, announcing his presence. "You're looking a little pale. You got morning sickness too?" she teased.

"Something like that," he smiled wanly. "Where's my lovely woman?"

"In the ladies room losing her breakfast, I'm assuming. That girl needs some good old-fashioned protein," she observed.

"Good luck with that," Kel replied, heading toward the restrooms.

"Mmhmm…" Joyce folded her arms, watching him go.

***

Kel rapped lightly on the bathroom door.

"Echo, dearest… are you okay?" he called out.

"I'm fine," she answered weakly. He heard water running and waited until it stopped before trying again.

"Is there anything you need? Can I help?"

There was silence for a moment, then Echo opened the door, pale and with a sheen of sweat on her face. Her curly red hair was frizzy, and she leaned into her fiancé's strong embrace.

"I don't feel good," she sighed.

"Let's get you home," Kel brushed damp strands of hair back from her face.

"I can't go home, it's the middle of the work day," she protested.

"We'll take care of that," he assured her, propelling her gently toward the front of the shop, where Joyce was busy rearranging a candle display.

"Joyce, do you suppose that you could handle watching over both sides of the shop for the rest of the afternoon?" he asked, one arm supporting his limp fiancée.

"No problem at all," she nodded. "You go on home, Miss Echo, and don't worry about a thing."

"Joyce, you're a treasure. I'm giving you a raise," Echo murmured, her head against Kel's broad chest.

"You did that last week, ma'am, we're good," the lovely, mocha-skinned young woman chuckled. "I get to spend my days surrounded by books and smelling delicious candles. What more could a girl want?"

"Thank you so much, Joyce," Kel smiled appreciatively, guiding Echo from the store.

"Take care, Mr. Kel," she waved at the couple. "I'm gonna make her some ribs and disguise them as tofu, I swear," she murmured as they left the store.

**

Echo and Kel were nearly at her house before she realized how odd it was that her fiancé had stopped by in the middle of the work day.

"Shouldn't you be at the studio?" she asked, frowning.

"Yes," he nodded, keeping his eyes on the road.

"Then why are you here? I told you that you shouldn't worry about me so much, honey. I'll be fine. I just need to drink some mushroom broth or something," she leaned her head back against the seat, placing her hand on his knee as he drove.

"There's something that I'd like to discuss with you, my darling girl," he replied, not looking at her.

"Are you okay? Is something wrong?" she sat up, concerned.

"I just have a lot on my mind," he hedged, and she immediately knew something was wrong. Kel was a master of conversation, and usually loved nothing more than to share his thoughts. Seeing him quiet and pensive was more than a bit unsettling.

"Pull over," Echo demanded, putting her hand over her mouth.

Kel swerved over onto the shoulder, and she leaned out of the car, dry heaving as her concerned fiancé stroked her back and held her hair. When the spasms passed, she sat back against the seat weakly, her eyes closed.

"I'm so sorry you're not feeling well," Kel lifted her hand and kissed it softly.

"I just want to go home," she moaned, not bothering to open her eyes.

"We're almost there, sweetie. Do you feel well enough to get back on the road?"

Echo nodded, refastening her seat belt and groaning a bit at the contact with her tummy.

"You poor thing," Kel murmured. "Let's get you home."

***

After Kel got his weak and weary fiancée settled on her sofa with a cup of herbal tea and a handful of soda crackers, he sat down next to her and took her hands in his.

"What is it?" she put her cup down, and stared at him, worried.

The artist sighed, and gazed at her as though he was trying to find just the right words.

"Did you change your mind?" she whispered, her lower lip trembling.

"Change my mind? About what?" Kel was baffled.

"About marrying me and having a baby and all of that? Is this scaring you? Is it too much? Am I not what you expected?" she asked tremulously, her eyes welling with tears. Clearly hormones were trumping common sense at the moment.

"Oh love, how can you even ask that?" he chided gently, pulling her into his arms to ease her fears. "Nothing in this world could change the way that I feel about you," he soothed, letting her snuffling wet the front of his shirt for a bit.

When her tears had subsided, he drew back a bit, and tilted her chin up for a chaste kiss.

"I love you, dearest, and because I love you, I'm hoping that you'll be very understanding about what I need to tell you," he began, stroking her cheek.

Echo's eyes widened, and she dabbed the tears from her face, staring at him with trepidation.

"Okay…"

"I had a visitor at my house this morning."

"Who?"

"A young man named Scott Hammond."

"Okay."

Echo was bracing herself for bad news and wondering what on earth he was going to tell her.

"He's from Illinois, and his mother is missing."

"I'm confused as to why any of this is important," she frowned, hoping that her fuzzy pregnancy brain wasn't causing her to misunderstand something.

"He needs my help."

"He's from Illinois and he needs your help? Who is this guy?"

"He's… oh dear Echo… he's my son," Kel's eyes pleaded for her understanding.

CHAPTER FOUR

"He has a what?" Missy demanded, putting down her mug of coffee.

"A fifteen-year-old son named Scott," Echo replied, shaking her head and staring down into her oatmeal.

She had met Missy at the cupcake shop, *Cupcakes in Paradise*, and had expressly forbidden her fiancé from joining them because she desperately needed some quality "girl time" with her best friend.

"Why didn't he tell you about him?"

"He had no idea. Apparently his girlfriend found out that she was pregnant, broke up with him and left town. He says the boy looks just like him," Echo poked her spoon into the tasty mushy goo that Missy had made, not eating a bite.

Missy reached over and squeezed her friend's hand.

"How are you feeling about all of this?" she asked.

Echo shrugged her shoulders.

"Well, it seems to me that now that he knows Scott exists, he should help him. I don't know why the boy's mother decided to keep the secret from Kel, but the cat's out of the bag now, and he can be a part of his life. He *should* be part of his life."

"How did I know you'd say something wonderful like that?" her friend grinned proudly.

"Wonderful? Hardly. It's just the right thing to do," was the pragmatic reply.

"Well, I'm still going to think of you as an amazing human being. Not all women would have taken the news so well," Missy pointed out.

"Everyone has a past. Kel just happens to have a past that produced a child. I was incredibly lucky, or that would be my story too. If Scott is a part of Kel, I'm sure that I'll love him."

"When do you meet him?"

"Tonight. I'm kind of nervous."

"I can't even imagine," Missy shook her head.

"I'm hoping that we all get along well and that we can involve him in the wedding."

"That would be wonderful. So, where is Scott's mother, and why is he here?"

"That's the thing… the reason that Scott searched for Kel in the first place is because his mother is missing," Echo sighed, finally taking a tiny bite of oatmeal, to Missy's delight.

"Missing? Oh my goodness, that's awful. Do the police have any leads?"

"He says that he can't go to the police because he feels like she might be with her boyfriend and that telling the police might put her in more danger."

"Yikes," Missy frowned. "So… how can Kel help?"

"You know Kel," Echo smiled faintly. "He's already been in contact with Jeanette's mom, and is going to see her later this afternoon."

"That had to have been an awkward conversation."

"I don't even want to think about it," Echo took another bite of the goo, washing it down with a sip of mint tea.

"So, is Scott staying with Kel now?"

"Yes, and I think that if Kel doesn't get any good info from Jeanette's mother, he'll probably be traveling back to Illinois with him to find out what's going on."

"Not to sound callous, but... what about the wedding?"

"It'll just have to wait for a while, I suppose. Some things are more important."

Missy tilted her head and regarded her friend fondly.

"You're pretty special, you know that?" she grinned.

"Nah, I'm just knocked up and patient," Echo winked.

***

"Hi, I'm Echo," she offered her hand to the shy teenager, who shook it and blushed.

"I'm Scott. You're really pretty."

"Like father, like son," she chuckled. "I like you already."

Kel came into the room with a tray of sandwiches. Echo looked quickly away from the platter, not wanting to trust her stomach at the moment.

"So, what did you find out?" she asked him after he and Scott had helped themselves.

"Very little. Jeanette's mom gave me the name of the boyfriend, and the firm that he works for, so I'll have some leads to follow up on, but I don't know how helpful they'll be. She definitely wants to see you, though, young man," he turned to Scott, who was chewing a huge mouthful of sandwich.

"Cool, I haven't seen Grandma in a long time. I've never been to her house, she always comes to see us."

"His grandparents live right here in the same town as you and they never…" Echo began, irate, until Kel shot her a warning look and held up his hand to interrupt.

"We'll talk about that later. In the meantime, let's just get to know each other a bit," he suggested diplomatically.

"Sure, of course," Echo nodded, forcing a smile for Scott's sake.

This was going to be a whole new world for her. Scott's resemblance to Kel was so striking, that there was no doubt in her mind that he was Kel's son. They even had some of the same mannerisms and expressions. The three of them chatted for the next several hours, getting to know each other, and Echo found Scott to be utterly delightful. His laugh was contagious, and, despite the fact that he was desperately worried about his mother, he actively participated in the conversation, which inevitably turned to theories and speculation on a pretty consistent basis.

"Is she going to be okay?" he asked at one point.

"We're going to do everything that we can to make sure that she is," Kel assured him, handing him another sandwich.

***

"So, what was he like?" Missy asked excitedly, taking a huge bite of her Mocha Cappuccino cupcake.

Echo was feeling a bit better today, and had been craving peanut butter, so Missy had whipped up a batch of vegan Peanut Butter cupcakes with creamy whipped peanut butter buttercream frosting, just for her. Echo savored every bite.

"He was charming, well spoken, really a sweet boy," she licked a smear of frosting from her thumb.

"So, basically a younger version of Kel?"

"Basically," Echo grinned. "It's really kind of fun seeing them together."

"I bet. So, what's happening with the investigation of his mother's disappearance?"

"Kel is checking into the boyfriend while Scott is over at his grandmother's house today. I just can't understand why the grandparents never said anything to Kel," Echo shook her head, taking another bite of cupcake.

"Maybe their daughter never told them who the father was," Missy suggested.

"Hopefully it's something like that. I'd hate to think that they knew all this time and never bothered to let him know that he had a son who looks just like him," she covered her mouth with her hand as she chewed.

"Are you going to go to Illinois with Kel if he goes?"

Echo shook her head again. "Probably not. I really don't want to be away from the candle shop that long. I know that Joyce will say that she can handle it, but it's not fair to her to make her work both shops full time every day."

"Have you thought about hiring a helper? You're going to have to take maternity leave, you know," Missy reminded her.

"Oh definitely. I figured I'd still work full time until I'm around seven months along, then I'll make Joyce the General Manager and hire an assistant for her."

"Good plan, although Joyce might prefer the title Manager General," she giggled. She loved Joyce's sassy, quick-witted nature, and could see her transitioning quite naturally into a leadership position.

"Oh gosh, she's the best. I seriously don't know what I'd do without her," Echo replied, drinking down an entire glass of iced water in a few large gulps.

"Whoa, slow down there, sister," Missy teased. "We don't want to see that coming back up again."

"The sickness comes and goes these days," her friend admitted. "I'm actually keeping way more things down now."

"Thank goodness. You were thin enough to begin with. I didn't want to have to start force-feeding you vegan cupcakes."

Echo chuckled. "You're not the only one. Joyce has been threatening to switch out my vegetables for soul food."

"Oooo! If she does, bring it over to me," Missy ordered playfully.

"I'll be sure to do that. Well, now that I've wolfed down my cupcake, I'd better get to the shop," she stood to go.

"All right, sugar, you take it easy and don't forget to eat," Missy hugged her friend.

"Okay Mom," Echo teased.

"Soon a sweet little angel is going to be calling you that, darlin,'" Missy's eyes welled up a bit.

"Stop! Emotion is not allowed," she held up her hand in protest. "I cry at the drop of a tissue these days, don't get me started," Echo warned, heading for the door.

"Love you, sugar."

"Love you, too," she sang out as the door closed behind her.

CHAPTER FIVE

Kel looked over the notes he had taken when he spoke with Scott's grandmother, Jean. Jeanette's boyfriend Stanton Vincenzo seemed to be the most normal, boring guy on the planet, at least on paper. He was an accountant at Parnelli and Sons Accounting, and had been since he'd graduated from a state school in the Chicago suburbs. The firm was located in the college town of Champaign— a couple of hours south of the Windy City—and, as far as Kel could tell, as they had no high-profile clients, they made most of their money during tax season.

The artist did an internet search on Stanton Vincenzo, and noted that he was around the same age as Jeanette. He searched for images and saw an average-looking, olive-skinned man with thick curly black hair. There wasn't much online about him, and he had no run-ins with the law, but Kel did notice that in the images section, there were photos of him with a handful of other men in exotic locales: on a yacht, at the beach, and apparently in several foreign countries. He wondered why an accountant would travel so much on business, and tried a few different searches to see if he could determine where

Stanton had been and when, but nothing showed up. Either the guy had nothing to hide, or he was really good at hiding it.

There was one photo which caught Kel's attention, simply because it featured Jeanette, with Stanton's arm slung casually over her shoulders, at what looked like a holiday party. She was still as lovely as she'd been the day that she'd left him without looking back, pleading a "need for space." Her once-flowing chestnut hair was now shoulder-length and fashioned into a suburban "mom cut;" although she was smiling, her eyes looked a bit sad. Or perhaps he was just projecting. The artist ran a hand through his hair and stretched. He needed to take a break and step back a bit. Time was of the essence, but he needed to tamp down the sadness that had risen up within him when he realized that Jeanette hadn't trusted him enough to tell him about Scott, and that she'd been alone all this time, raising their son. He hoped for his son's sake that she was okay, and he was prepared to travel to Illinois if he needed to.

Staring at the phone on his desk, he reached for the receiver, then drew his hand back. He had no desire to speak to Stanton Vincenzo; unfortunately, he didn't seem to have much of a choice. Sighing, he picked up the phone and dialed.

"Parnelli and Sons," a nasal voice on the other end of the phone sounded annoyed.

"Hello, may I speak with Stanton Vincenzo, please?" Kel asked pleasantly, tapping his pen nervously on his blotter.

"Who's calling please?"

Kel thought fast. Just in case Vincenzo did turn out to be a bad guy, he didn't want him knowing his name.

"Kelvin Phillips, I believe he's expecting my call," he said smoothly.

"One moment, please," the indifferent receptionist said, placing him immediately on hold.

"Mr. Phillips, thanks for the call, how can I help ya today?" a polite voice with a slight accent answered.

"Mr. Vincenzo?" Kel confirmed.

"You got me."

"I have a strange question for you, if you don't mind."

"No problem, Kelvin, shoot," Stanton said magnanimously. Kel could almost picture him twirling around in an executive chair, hands behind his head.

"Jeanette Hammond is my cousin," Kel swallowed. For some reason, her name sounded strange on his lips after so many years. "And she usually calls my mother, just to catch up, you know how women are, on Sundays. She hasn't called, and Ma is getting nervous. Jeanie mentioned that she'd been seeing you pretty regularly lately, so I thought you might have an idea of where she's hiding out, ya know?" he mirrored the accountant's conversational style.

Stanton chuckled. "Women," he sighed. "Yeah, I hear ya. I hate to tell ya, Kelvin, but I'm getting a little worried about the gal myself. I haven't heard from her in a while, and I know she's busy and all, but it's still making me wonder. I mean, not even a text, ya know?"

"Yeah, it is weird. When did you hear from her last?"

"Couple weeks ago. We had dinner downtown on Friday at a new Italian place, I dropped her off at home after, and I haven't heard from her since."

"That's when we stopped hearing from her too," Kel commiserated. "Well listen, thanks for your time Mr. Vincenzo."

"You bet, buddy. Hey, give me another call if you hear from her, all right?" Stanton asked.

"Will do, thanks for your time."

They hung up and Kel stared at his desk blotter, tapping a pen on the notepad in front of him. Stanton sounded like a genuinely nice guy, even if he didn't seem terribly worried about Jeanette. But then again, he knew how entirely independent his former girlfriend was—perhaps she had kept Vincenzo at arm's length like she had Kel. He sighed and dropped the pen in frustration. It looked like he was going to have to go to Champaign to track down some of Jeanette's coworkers and see if they knew anything helpful. According to her mother, Jeanette didn't really have girlfriends. She threw herself wholeheartedly into working and making a home for Scott; she only dated or went out with coworkers on rare occasions. It sounded like the years hadn't changed her much.

***

It had been a long time since Kel had been in an airport that was so small, pleasant and unassuming. Willard Airport in Champaign brought back memories of the good old days, prior to 9/11, when one could actually drive up to the curb in front of the terminal and pick up their friend, colleague, or loved one within minutes of them landing. There were perhaps half a dozen taxis parked out front, which was fortunate, because the only limo service in the area was completely booked with weddings and graduations. The drivers lounged against their cars and scurried to help with luggage when a customer approached. He didn't have to avail himself of their services, however, having rented a car, and the traffic was refreshingly light. There were no five-star hotels in town, so Kel had reserved a room in a brand-new four-star that was in the heart of the picturesque downtown.

This was Jeanette's world, and he tried to imagine her here, eating at the cute, casual restaurants, weaving through clumps of grad students to make her way to the funky coffee shops, or having a drink with friends on one of the outdoor patios along the main strip. Champaign was roughly the size of Calgon, but its laid-back, Midwest feel had Kel anticipating a relaxed stay as he tackled the unpleasant task at hand.

Jeanette worked for a local real estate office, as an agent. Kel had no idea how a realtor had happened to meet and date an accountant, but he certainly intended to find out. Driving south and west of downtown, he found a quaint, upscale strip mall which housed bars, restaurants, a coffee shop, and various professional offices, one of which was the real estate company at which Jeanette worked. He parked out front, and put on his most "I'm-an-innocent-home-buyer" smile and headed into the cool, tastefully furnished interior of the firm.

"Good morning, sir. How may I help you?" a stunning blond twenty-something receptionist asked.

"Hello. I'm from out of town, and interested in taking a look at some homes, in case I get transferred out here. A friend of mine referred me to Jeanette Hammond. Is she available?" Kel asked pleasantly.

Clearly the blonde had been coached well, her response was immediate and professional.

"Oh, I'm sorry, Jeanette isn't going to be in the office for a few days, would you like to speak with a member of her team?"

"I'm sorry... her team?" he asked, not wanting to sound too eager. She had offered him exactly what he needed, a chance to speak with someone close to Jeanette.

"Yes sir. Jeanette is a member of a team, and they help each other's clients when a team member is on vacation, or has too many closings stacked up, that sort of thing," the blonde smiled sweetly.

"Well, that's very efficient," Kel nodded. "So, if I end up buying a home, Jeanette will still get the commission and all of that?"

"Yes sir, the team has ways of handling those situations to make it fair to all involved. If you'd like to have a seat, I can get Rhonda out here to get you started," she gestured to the waiting room.

"Perfect, thank you," he replied, moving to sit in one of the subtly stylish faux suede chairs.

The receptionist got on the phone to summon Rhonda to the front, and Kel picked up a real estate book, flipping through the pages idly. He spied a dish of individually wrapped, creamy, rich, hard caramels, and popped one into his mouth. He'd forgotten to eat breakfast before starting off on his little adventure, and didn't want the realtor to have to hear his stomach growling. A tall, buxom woman, roughly Jeanette's age, with hair dyed an interesting shade of copper, approached him, hand extended.

"Hello there," she trilled. "I'm Rhonda Cooper."

"Kelvin, Kelvin Phillips," he shook her hand, talking around the candy in his mouth.

"Well, it's a pleasure to meet you, Kelvin. Won't you please come with me?" she waited for him to rise from his chair, then led him toward the inner sanctum in a cloud of pleasant perfume.

"So Denise tells me that you're one of Jeanette's referrals and that you might like to see some houses today, is that correct?" she asked, immediately getting down to business.

Kel seated himself in a club chair across the wide grey Formica desk from her.

"Yes, that's right," he nodded.

"Would you like some coffee?" she asked.

"That would be great, thank you."

Rhonda pressed a button on her intercom, requesting that Denise bring coffee, then folded her heavily baubled hands in front of her, and regarded Kel with a friendly smile. He tried to not be distracted by the sheer number and size of her accessories.

"So, tell me a bit about your situation, then we'll dive into what you're looking for in a home, and then we can go see some houses."

Prepared to ferret information out of the realtor, Kel hadn't anticipated that she might have some questions for him; luckily, he fabricated pretty easily on the fly.

"I'm living in Florida, and there's a possibility that I may be spending a great deal of time in the Midwest, so I thought that I should probably look into purchasing a home out here."

"I see," she nodded. "Well, you're in for a treat. There are so many lovely homes on the market, and the prices can't be beat. So, how do you know Jeanette?" she asked, a slight hint of suspicion coloring her tone.

"I don't, actually," he shrugged. It was true, he had no idea what his former sweetheart was like now. "A friend of mine knows her really well, and when he heard that I was coming out here, he recommended her."

Rhonda nodded, and there was a faint knock on the door, as Denise, the beautiful blonde, came in bearing a tray with two steaming mugs of coffee, cream and sugar, and a plate of peanut butter cookies. Kel's stomach growled audibly and the women chuckled.

"Should I bring more cookies?" Denise teased, on her way out.

"I'll let you know," Kel grinned, taking a sip of his coffee.

"So, who's your friend... the one who gave the referral?" Rhonda asked, seemingly preoccupied with stirring cream into her coffee.

"Oh... Scott, uh... Malcolm Scott. He's a good guy."

Rhonda wrote down something on a pad that was hidden behind her computer monitor.

"We like to keep track of these things," she explained, seeming satisfied with his answer. "Referrals are very important in this business."

"I can imagine," Kel nodded.

They chatted about what Kel was looking for in a home, which was easy for him—he simply described the features that he had in his home in Calgon.

"Well, the need for a pool really narrows the market pretty significantly," Rhonda clickety-clicked away on her computer, frowning.

"What if we look at properties that have room for a pool, should I decide to put one in?" he asked helpfully.

"That makes life easier," she agreed, brightening. "Okay, since you want to go out and look right away, we'll look at the ones that are vacant for now, then I can make appointments to see those that are occupied for tomorrow, how does that sound?"

Kel didn't want to get locked into having his time taken up, particularly if the realtor wasn't helpful in giving him information about Jeanette.

"I'm not sure just yet what commitments I'm going to have for tomorrow, so we can go look today, and then, perhaps I can text you with my availability in the morning?"

"That's fine," she agreed, hitting the print button on her computer and glancing at her watch. "That means we have four to see today. If there's any way that you can let me know tonight, rather than tomorrow morning, so that I can make appointments for us, that would really help me out," she blinked at him.

"I'll try my best," he gave her what he hoped was a charming smile.

"Great. Go ahead and bring your coffee with you, and let's get started," she stood, grabbed her purse from under her desk, and headed for the door.

***

"So, you've never actually met Jeanette?" Rhonda asked, when they were on their way to the first house. Her oversized sunglasses not only hid her eyes, but most of her face as well, and her rings glittered in the sunlight.

"Nope, I haven't," he mentally crossed his fingers at the lie. "What's she like?" That was a genuine question, he was curious.

"Oh, she's lovely, inside and out, and talk about a great realtor… she really goes above and beyond for her clients," Rhonda reached over and cranked up the A/C, effectively dissipating the heavily perfumed air in her car.

"Nice. Her husband must feel like a lucky guy," he probed, hoping that he wasn't being too obvious.

"Oh honey, Jeanette isn't married. She doesn't have time for men, she's all about the job. Although she has gone out with a couple of guys lately, and just between you and me, I can't tell what her taste in men is—the two guys are as different as night and day," she confided, taking a quick but meaningful glance at Kel over the tops of her gigantic sunglasses.

"Really?" he grinned, trying to put Rhonda at ease so she'd keep going.

She nodded, pursing her lips.

"You betcha. One is a respectable accountant, who seems boring, but, you know… stable. The other one is movie-star good-looking, but… he's a mechanic," she whispered. "Not that there's anything wrong with that, but Jeanie just doesn't seem to be a grease-under-the-nails kinda gal, you know?"

"They have amazing cleaning products to protect against that these days," Kel shrugged.

"Well yes, but that's not exactly my point. She's well... polished, sophisticated, you know? It just seems strange."

"Maybe he brings out a hidden wild side or something," the artist suggested mildly, with a chuckle.

Rhonda laughed, nodding. "We've all taken a walk on the wild side, haven't we?"

"Indeed," Kel agreed, wondering how he might be able to get the mechanic's name.

The rest of the afternoon passed very pleasantly, with Kel and Rhonda viewing some lovely homes, but without him gathering any more valuable info. She gave him her card, and told him to call her when he had his schedule for the next day figured out. Feeling that he had probably tapped the extent of her knowledge about the very private Jeanette Hammond, he probably wouldn't be in touch, but promised that he would.

Settling back into his room after having a lovely drink at a funky, upscale tapas restaurant across the street from his hotel, Kel checked his phone and realized that he had forgotten to turn the ringer back on after his time with Rhonda. There was a voicemail from a number that he didn't recognize.

"Hey Kelvin... Stanton Vincenzo here. I got your number from the caller ID on my phone. There's something I forgot to tell you that might help us find your cousin Jeanette. Give me a call when you get this. Thanks."

Kel's eyes went wide and he hit the Call Back button.

CHAPTER SIX

Missy had taken sensitive, artistic Grayson Myers under her wing when she first hired him to work at her shop in LaChance, Louisiana; the pale, tattooed youth, with long dark hair and soulful eyes, had been like a son to her ever since. Petaluma, his birth mother, was a raging alcoholic who had begun throwing him out of the house since he was around nine years old. She wasn't a huge part of his life now that he was an adult, but he'd requested that she be able to attend his wedding.

"Of course your mama can come, honey. We'll have a room for her here at the inn," Missy assured him, trying to feel optimistic about the prospect of having Petaluma under her roof.

"Oh no!" Grayson exclaimed. "You really don't have to do that Mrs. B. I don't think that Mom will fit in there…"

"Oh, darlin, now you know we'll do our absolute best to make her feel right at home," Missy protested.

"No, that's not what I mean. You know what she's like, Mrs. B., I mean, I love her and all, but I don't want her to embarrass anyone. She should really just go to a hotel or something," he insisted.

"Well, why don't we just ask her what she'd prefer to do? That seems like the right way to handle it."

There was an audible sigh from Grayson's end. "I suppose so," he said uncertainly.

"Good then. I'm so excited to see you two in a couple of months," she grinned from ear to ear.

"We can't wait," the shy young man confessed. "I've really missed you and Miss Echo."

"Oh honey, I haven't told you her good news…"

Missy told Grayson about Echo's engagement and delicate condition and the thoughtful young man came up with an idea that she hadn't considered. They spent the next half hour or so plotting and planning, both of them delighted with their newly created secret.

"Remember, don't tell her," Grayson admonished one more time before hanging up. "This has to be a surprise."

"You got it, honey. I wouldn't miss the look on her face for anything in the world," Missy chuckled.

Just as she hung up the phone, still smiling, Echo came in the front door of the cupcake shop, looking far less weary than she had been previously.

"Hey, darlin!" Missy put the phone down on the counter and gave her best friend a hug. "You're looking better."

"It's amazing how good you feel when your stomach actually decides to keep the food that you put in it," she quipped.

"Well, yay! Think you're finally getting the hang of this pregnancy thing?"

"I wouldn't go that far, but it does seem to be getting more bearable."

"That's a good thing. Can you handle a cupcake? I have some vegan Coconut Cremes..." Missy tempted her friend.

"Coconut??? Oh, that is the magic word! I can't get enough of it lately, bring me two please," Echo was delighted.

"And a cup of herbal tea?"

"I want coffee," she pouted.

"You can't have coffee, darlin," Missy blinked at her.

"I still want it," was the glum reply. "Fine, I'll have tea. Just pick something that'll go well with the coconut."

"You got it, sugar."

Missy was back in a flash with cupcakes for both of them, coffee for her and tea for Echo, all on a pretty little silver tray.

"Have you heard anything from Kel?"

"Yeah, he's found out a few things after talking to one of Jeanette's friends, and he said he got a strange call from the accountant boyfriend, but he's still up there digging. I wish I could join him," she mused.

"Why don't you go then? Joyce can watch the store, right?"

"Of course she could. That girl runs a tight ship," Echo smiled. "But I'm honestly not feeling up to traveling, and I can't just leave Scott here by himself."

"Oh, that's right," Missy nodded, remembering that the boy had stayed behind. "Why didn't Kel take him back to Illinois?"

"Because he figured that if something bad has happened to his mother, Scott might be in danger, so he's safe and sound housesitting while Kel is away."

"I sure hope his mama is okay," Missy said, taking a sip of her coffee.

"Me, too."

"I wonder if Kel needs any help…"

"I never thought of that," Echo exclaimed. "I can't go to Illinois to help Kel, but you could."

"That's a great idea. Things are a bit slow right now, so I could have Spencer watch the shop and Maggie can handle the inn," she nodded.

"When does Spencer leave for his new assignment?" Echo asked sadly.

Spencer Bengal, a young, handsome Marine veteran who served as the inn's handyman, had been secretly working undercover, having been hired by Chas's family to protect the eldest heir to the Beckett estate. The Marine had saved them from several dangerous situations and had become like a member of the family. When Echo started making her custom candles, he'd jumped right in to help her pump up her inventory, and he often presided over the cupcake counter in Missy's shop when she had to run errands.

When Chas and Missy had made the decision to sell the inn and cupcake shop a few short weeks ago, so that they could move to New York, enabling Chas to take over Beckett Holdings, Spencer had informed them that he'd been reassigned, a fact which broke their hearts. No one knew the details as yet, including Spencer, and they were all dreading the day that his smile no longer warmed their lives.

"We still don't know," Missy said softly. "I'm hoping that something changes... I don't know what we'll do without him."

"You should go to Champaign and see if Kel needs help," Echo changed the subject abruptly, before tears threatened. She was having a hard time dealing with the emotional highs and lows brought on by pregnancy.

"Should I call and ask him if he even wants my help?" Missy worried.

"Heck, no," Echo shook her head and grinned. "He'll just tell you that everything is fine and progressing nicely, you know how he is. The man wouldn't ask for help if you paid him to," she sighed, missing her fiancé.

"There's that. Are you sure that you're not just sending me out there to keep an eye on him for you?" she teased.

"No, but I'm hoping that with two of you working to find Jeanette, she'll turn up quicker and he can come home and rub my feet," Echo giggled. "I really miss him."

"I'm sure you do, sugar. Well, let me talk to Chas. I can probably catch a flight tomorrow."

"You're the best," Echo hugged her fearless friend.

CHAPTER SEVEN

Missy stared out the window of the airplane, brooding a bit. Chas hadn't approved that the police hadn't been contacted about Kel's missing ex-girlfriend, but had relented a bit when Missy said she'd be going up there to convince him to do just that. It wasn't a lie— she planned to encourage him to go to the police, but she would be by his side investigating in the meantime.

Per Echo's request, she hadn't notified Kel that she was coming, but was nearly certain that he wouldn't have a problem with her being there. She knew which hotel he was in, and which room, and had booked a suite across the hall from him. It was kind of thrilling to think that soon she'd be in a totally unfamiliar place trying to solve what might be a kidnapping. She hoped that Scott's mother had simply needed time for herself and had just been careless in communicating, but a sense of dread overcame her every time she thought about it. What mother would leave her teenaged son for weeks without a word?

She checked into the brand-new downtown hotel and freshened up a bit before going across the hall and knocking on Kel's door. When the artist didn't answer immediately, she decided to take a walk around the downtown area and explore a bit. The city was so uncrowded and laid-back that she felt immediately at home, and decided to stop at a quaint little hipster coffee shop for a snack before heading back. Across the street was a bustling bar and grill that had the most amazing smell of grilled burgers emanating from beneath its awnings. She felt a bit guilty admitting it, but this time away from the inn and the cupcake shop and all of her various daily activities felt like a little vacation, so she took her time, finishing every last drop of her latte and curried egg salad sandwich before heading back to the hotel.

***

"Hi Stanton, it's Kel— vin Phillips," Kel stuttered, forgetting for a moment that he was undercover. "I got your message. You said you remembered something about Jeanie?"

"Oh, yeah, hey Kelvin, how ya doin? Yeah, I remembered that she was having car troubles before I stopped hearing from her, and she said that when she dropped off the car, the mechanic was hitting on her. I mean, stuff like that happens to her all the time, she's a doll, ya know… but, this guy weirded her out. Might be worth checking out," Vincenzo explained.

"At this point, I'm thinking that she probably just took a trip to the Bahamas to forget about it all for a while, but my ma really wants me to try to find her," Kel did his best to sound nonchalant. "You got any idea who the mechanic is?" His pen was poised over a notepad, and he was having a bit of fun mirroring Stanton Vincenzo's speech patterns.

"Nah, she didn't say. She felt silly making a big deal over it. But I'm sure if your ma has a key to her house, you can get in there and maybe find a receipt or something," Stanton suggested.

Kel had been trying to stay away from invading Jeanette's private space, but what her boyfriend said made sense. There might be clues there that would lead him to her.

"That's a thought," he played it cool, not wanting to let Stanton know that he'd definitely be going to Jeanie's place. "Maybe ma can go over and look. I feel kinda weird about it. Like we're all going to be embarrassed when she comes back tanned and relaxed and we were all worried for nothing."

"I hear ya, man. Let's hope that's all it is. Lemme know if you find anything."

"Sure will. And thanks for the tip—I appreciate it."

"You betcha, anything to help."

After pressing the End button on his phone, Kel jotted down some notes and looked in his wallet for the piece of paper that Scott had given him with Jeanette's address on it. He felt caught up in some kind of weird dream. Just a few days ago, he'd been a single, childless man, and now he was about to be married and had one son and a child on the way. The artist nearly jumped out of his skin when he heard a soft knock on his hotel room door, and made his way soundlessly to the peephole, shocked at who was standing on the other side.

"Hey darlin," Missy greeted him with a warm hug.

"Is my lovely bride-to-be in the habit of sending chaperones these days?" he joked, genuinely glad to see a familiar face.

"Nope, I'm just too darn nosy to stay put."

"You realize that we might both be in danger now?" Kel raised his eyebrows.

"Do you have any idea how often I've heard that line?" Missy replied wryly.

"Come on in. I have a fully-stocked mini-bar, so you can hydrate while I bring you up to speed," he invited, closing the door behind his fiancée's best friend.

While Missy drank two bottles of water and munched on a handful of trail mix, he told her about his conversations with Rhonda the realtor and Stanton Vincenzo. She nodded, taking it all in.

"Sounds like we need to find the mechanic. That seems to be the common thread in both conversations so far," she mused.

"That was my thought as well," Kel agreed. "And you being here might actually make my story about being Jeanette's cousin more plausible."

"I hardly look like your mother, Kel," Missy grumbled.

"Clearly," he rolled his eyes. "But if anyone is watching her place and see a man and a woman go in, it makes it look like we could be relatives of hers, rather than just me going in as a single, stalking male," he pointed out.

"Oh. Good point."

"Does Chas know you're here?" Kel raised an eyebrow.

"He absolutely does. And if he should happen to call, I'm trying my very best to talk you into going to the police with your concerns," she gave him a pointed look, which made him chuckle.

"Why is it that all the women in my life are adventurous, headstrong types?" he teased.

"Because you're a lucky man," Missy shot back, not missing a beat. "Now, how are we going to get into Jeanette's house?"

"Through the back door. Scott gave me a key."

"Should we wait until it's dark, so no one will see us?"

"Do you want to face potentially dangerous people who might show up in the dark or in broad daylight?"

"You do have a point… so we're going now?"

"I think it's best. The sooner we get this over with, the sooner we can get back home. Do you have a hotel yet?"

"I'm right across the hall."

"Of course you are," Kel chuckled. "Let's go see what we can find."

***

Jeanette and Scott lived in a modest home that was close enough to a golf course to have all the amenities of an area with manicured lawns and beautifully kept homes, but not so close that the structures were gated and imposing. This, unfortunately, was the type of neighborhood where neighbors knew each other and knew who belonged and who didn't.

"Oh boy, people are going to know that we're strangers around here," Missy remarked, as a man watering his flowers raised a hand in greeting. She smiled and waved back. "So, we're supposed to be Jeanette's cousins?"

"Yup. Since I... knew her, just let me do the talking and we should be fine if we encounter anyone," Kel advised.

"Roger wilco," Missy nodded, taking in the lush green lawns and colorful flowers around her. They'd driven past acres upon acres of cornfields to get to the neighborhood, and the place was decidedly different from Florida, but had its own down-home charm.

Kel turned to look at her, blinking once before returning his eyes to the road.

"What? I saw it in a police show once," she grinned.

"Ah, here we are, 3311 Pond's Edge," he pulled into the long driveway of the well-kept ranch-style home.

"How is her yard so perfect if she's been gone for a couple of weeks?" Missy wondered, admiring the landscaping.

"She must have a lawn service or something," Kel guessed, turning off the engine.

"Since you're parked in the driveway, we might as well go in the front door."

"That's the plan," he said quietly, staring at the house with an unfathomable look on his face.

"Well, come on then," Missy said, itching to get inside so that they could find clues.

The couple held their breath as Kel jiggled the key in the lock until it finally clicked open.

"No alarm system?" Missy wondered.

"Apparently, Jeanette feels very safe here."

"Well, let's hope that she was correct in that assumption. Should we split up to make this go faster?"

"Absolutely," Kel nodded. "Scott mentioned an office, I'll start there. You should check the kitchen and Jeanette's room."

"Sounds like a plan," Missy agreed, turning right to head into the kitchen.

There was a corkboard over the small kitchen desk. Missy assessed the board, its calendar, and the plethora of sticky notes on it. She lightly ran her finger over them to see if any of them contained information that might be relevant. There was one that said "pick up car" that was tacked to a Saturday, a little over two weeks ago. Missy took a picture of it with her phone, holding up the edge of it so that the date showed. The drawer of the little desk held pens, pencils, notepads and not much else, so after looking through the rest of the kitchen drawers, she headed to Jeanette's bedroom.

She first went to the nightstand by the bed and found that apparently Jeanette suffered from seasonal allergies and possibly asthma, as the drawer contained an inhaler, along with a couple of paperback novels, a half-eaten bag of gummi bears, and a jar of chewable vitamins. A further search of the room turned up nothing, until Missy went into the long, narrow walk-in closet. Just inside the door on a small chest of drawers was a purse. There were several purses tucked neatly into slots near the top shelf of the custom closet, but this one looked as though it had been placed there recently. Feeling a bit guilty, Missy peeked inside and found all of the things typically found in an everyday purse. Keys, wallet with credit cards and money, various receipts and odds and ends that would typically be present in a woman's purse were all there, causing Missy's heart to drop to her stomach. No woman would leave home for an extended amount of time without her purse. Jeanette Hammond wasn't on vacation, she was missing.

"Kel," she called softly, turning around and letting out a startled scream when she bumped into him as he entered the closet. "Oh my gosh, I…" she started to say, when he put a finger to his lips, his eyes darting to the window, where Missy saw a car that had just pulled up.

Her eyes went wide and she looked about frantically, searching for a place to hide.

"Follow me," he whispered, moving quickly from the closet.

He made his way swiftly through the kitchen, and practically dragged Missy down the basement stairs, just as they heard the doorbell ring. The basement was finished in a style that suggested it hadn't been updated since the house was built. It was tasteful, and well maintained, but true to the period with olive, mustard, and blaze-orange décor, but Missy couldn't focus on the room because Kel was busy trying to locate a suitable hiding place as they heard the front door creak open above them.

"Hello?" Rhonda the realtor called out tentatively. "Jeanie... are you home?"

Missy and Kel ducked into a dark niche between the utility closet and the washer and dryer, in an unfinished part of the basement. They heard the click-click of the realtor's heels in the foyer.

"Who is that, and why does she have a key?" Missy whispered, trying to control her breathing.

Kel placed a finger to his lips and shook his head, shushing her. They heard footsteps as Rhonda wandered around the house, occasionally calling out Jeanette's name. Missy thought her heart would pound right out of her chest when the clickety-clacking heels stopped right in front of the basement door.

"Jeanie? You doing laundry?" she called out.

Missy gave Kel a wide-eyed panicked look, and he squeezed her shoulder, putting a finger to his lips again. There was a pregnant pause, during which Missy thought that surely Rhonda could hear her heartbeat all the way upstairs, but then the basement door shut and she made her way out of the house. They waited until they heard her car start up and pull away before breathing a sigh of relief.

"Well, it looks like I have to turn the rental car in today," Kel sighed, shaking his head.

"Why?"

"Because it was sitting in the driveway when Rhonda the realtor drove up. If she's any kind of friend, she's probably calling the police about it right now and reporting the license plate number."

"Oh, right," Missy frowned. "Well, I rented a car too, so we can turn yours in and use mine."

"Now we're under the gun to figure out where Jeanette is and what's going on before the police figure out that I'm here pretending to be someone else while I investigate a disappearance. That was a careless mistake, I should've parked blocks away."

Missy put a hand on his arm. "It is what it is. Did you find anything?"

They hurried up the steps and Kel spoke over his shoulder.

"Yes, fortunately I found the name and number of the man who may be the mechanic that was supposed to be fixing her car. Did you find anything?" he asked, looking carefully into the street before carefully closing the door behind them, using the sleeve of his button-down as a glove.

They got into the car and pulled out cautiously, making certain that Rhonda's car was nowhere to be seen.

"Yes, I did. This," she held up Jeanette's purse, which she'd been carrying since Kel found her in the closet.

"Let's hope it helps. I'm going to drive straight to the airport to drop off the car, then we should take separate cabs back to the hotel," he said, strategizing. "Once we get there, you go through the purse, and I'll try to track down what info I can on the mechanic. With any luck, we'll be able to send you over there to pose as Jeanie's cousin, so that you can try to flirt with him and make him talk."

Missy's eyes widened. "Me?"

"Yes, I've already talked to her boyfriend and Rhonda, and they both mentioned the mechanic. I don't want them catching on to the fact that someone is looking into Jeanette's disappearance."

"Yeah, that makes sense," she nodded pensively. "All right, let's do this. We have to find out what happened to your son's mom."

CHAPTER EIGHT

Spencer Bengal vigorously polished the already sparkling countertop at Cupcakes in Paradise, deep in thought. He'd dedicated the last few years of his life to serving the Beckett family as a private security guard for Detective Chas Beckett, the eldest son and heir to the family empire and fortune. Chas hadn't known that the handsome young man who was hired to be the handyman at the Beach House Bed and Breakfast was actually sent there by Chalmers, Chas's father's former valet who now ran Beckett Holdings since Chas had refused the position. He'd discovered most of Spencer's true identity only recently, and was a bit put out to discover that he'd been secretly watched and protected for years.

Now, however, Spencer's situation had changed dramatically. Part of his training for the Beckett private security force had been with a special unit in the Marines which had performed covert and top-secret missions, in conjunction with a civilian dark ops organization. The understanding with the dark ops organization had been that they would provide training for Spencer, as well as a handful of other young men, in exchange for the right to call them

81

into service for matters of national security. Spencer and one of his brothers-in-arms, a now-scarred young man named Janssen, had been successful in evading the dark ops organization. Both had changed their names and adopted new identities in order to stay out of the clutches of the often dangerous organization, and now both worked to protect Chas and Missy.

Janssen, who had never been able to assimilate to civilian life after returning from Afghanistan, lived off the land in the Florida swamps, and always seemed to show up when Spencer needed backup. He'd contacted his handsome friend earlier in the week to let him know that Steve Arnold, their former supervisor from dark ops, had been making plans for a new operation that would involve some of the special skills that Spencer had acquired in training. How Janssen received his intel was a mystery, but he was almost never wrong, and that had Spencer worried. He couldn't protect Chas if he had to go to some foreign country to fulfill his obligation to dark ops. And then there was Izzy…

As if his thoughts had conjured her, the beautiful young best-selling author breezed into the cupcake shop.

"Hey you," he grinned, hoping that his smile was convincing.

"Hey yourself," she stood on her tiptoes and kissed his cheek from across the counter. "I needed to take a break from the bloodbath that I was writing about, so I decided to come visit you and have a cupcake." This sweet, delicate creature wrote some currently highly successful horror novels, and chose to live in Calgon to hide away from her publisher and fans. Her hazel eyes sparkled merrily, and she looked so beautiful to him in that moment that he didn't want to spoil her mood and decided to pretend that all was well. He should've known better.

"What's wrong?" she demanded, raising an eyebrow. She too, had recently found out what her current love interest did for a living, and was not at all happy about the fact that it was his job to regularly put himself in danger on behalf of others. "Grab me a Cocoa Mocha, a Salted Caramel, and a cup of coffee, then you're going to tell me what's going on," she ordered.

Wordlessly he reached for the cupcakes, placing them and a steaming mug of coffee on a tray, and sat down across from a now serious Izzy.

"This must be bad," she murmured, not looking at him, but swiping her forefinger through the caramel sauce on the top of her cupcake and licking it from her finger.

"Not necessarily..." Spencer hedged, glad that she wasn't looking at him at the moment.

Izzy took a massive bite of the cupcake, glaring at him as she did so. "Out wif it," she mumbled through the gooey richness, shielding her chewing from him with the back of her crumb-sprinkled hand.

"If I disappear, you have to believe that it's not my fault," he sighed, running a hand through his thick black hair.

She stopped chewing for a moment, then slowly continued, blinking at him in disbelief. Picking up her coffee, she washed the enormous bite down with the dark liquid and set the cup down again, slowly, deliberately.

"That sounded like a line from one of the victims in my novels," she said quietly.

"Unfortunately, there always exists the possibility that I might meet the same end as some of your characters do," he admitted, covering her hand with his and searching her eyes, hoping that she wouldn't bolt and never look back. "I just... wanted you to know."

"Wanted me to know what?" Izzy drew her hand back impatiently. "You haven't told me anything. I have no idea why you might just disappear," she accused.

"There are... powerful people who say they need my help. I don't want to do whatever they want me to do, but I may not have a choice," Spencer replied carefully.

"Who? Who wants you to do something that you don't want to do?" she demanded, the edge of tears in her voice.

"I can't..."

"You can't tell me, I know," she interrupted impatiently. "You can never tell me anything that's going on in your life, other than that you're some kind of security guard or spy or superhero or something. Who calls the shots in your life, Spence? The President?" she mumbled, trying not to cry.

When the strong and mysterious young man in front of her simply stared at her, his gaze never wavering, realization dawned.

"You work for the government? That's it, isn't it? You work for some secret government organization. Please tell me that you don't kill people, I couldn't take it if I thought that you kill people," she whimpered, totally distraught.

Spencer glanced about, as though he was afraid that they might be overheard. He leaned closer and spoke in a low voice.

"It's not that simple," he replied. "And I have to ask you to never say anything like that again. You could be putting your life in danger if the wrong people hear you speaking that way," he warned, his eyes concerned, his fingertips resting lightly on her arm.

Izzy took a deep breath, sat up straight, and pushed her cupcakes and coffee away, seeming to come to a decision. Before she could speak, his heart thudding as he wondered what she might say, Spencer laid his heart bare before her.

"Izzy, my sweet girl... I have to leave Calgon. I don't know where I'll end up yet, and I'm hoping that it may only be temporary, but I want you to come with me. Your safety is already at risk because of what you know about me, and I'd like to keep you close, not just so that I can keep you safe, but because I want you to be wherever I am. I know I've been distant, and afraid to share, but I really care about you, Izzy. Will you be with me? No matter what it takes?" he asked, reaching up to tenderly brush a tear from her pale, creamy cheek.

The agonized look in her eyes gave him his answer, crushing his soul before she ever opened her mouth.

"I... I'm sorry, Spencer," tears began to fall in earnest. "I can't do this anymore. We'd never have a normal life. I don't want to be looking over my shoulder, wondering if the boogeyman is going to get me when I leave the grocery store. I don't want to think that when the wind blows through the trees it's really an army of men surrounding my house. I'm sorry Spence, I care about you... I really do, but I can't live like that," she shook her head and gathered her purse, standing to go.

Spencer rose quickly from his chair and moved to embrace her.

"Wait," he said urgently, but she pushed him away, backing away slowly and shaking her head.

"No, Spencer. Just... no. I can't. I'm sorry," she sobbed. "No goodbyes, no kisses, it's better this way," she turned and fled, leaving him standing in the cupcake shop, his eyes moist, his jaw flexing with raw emotion.

He hadn't allowed himself to become close to a woman in a very long time, and this was why. He gathered up her cupcakes and still-warm coffee cup, put them on the tray, and moved to the kitchen in a daze.

CHAPTER NINE

Before Scott Hammond's mother disappeared, he'd had no idea who his birth father was, and he'd been surprised to learn that Kel wasn't just an accomplished artist, but was world-renowned, and… well… rich. His head still swiveled when he walked through Kel's spacious, gallery-like home. His mother's house in Champaign was nice, but nothing even close to the artist's spotlessly clean contemporary home. To say that the teenager had been intimidated at first would be an extreme understatement, but he'd managed to find his way around the large home, and stayed mostly in the den, playing video games and watching TV, while waiting for news from his father.

Scott had been lulled into a state of complacency in the huge alarm-protected house, so he moved through his days still worried about his mother, but feeling safe. Echo often came over to keep him company, and he'd grown to like the free-spirited redhead, despite the fact that she was nothing like his mother. She brought him groceries and fixed him vegan meals that he was surprised to discover were quite tasty, she took him to her cozy little cottage across town and showed him how to make hand-dipped and sculpted candles, an endeavor which he was surprisingly good at, and hung out watching movies with him at Kel's house.

An hour or two after Echo had said goodnight and gone home, locking the door and setting the alarm behind her, Scott startled awake, his heart pounding. Kel's stairway was a modern masterpiece of teak and steel that looked like it just floated its way toward the second and third floors, and the teenager swore that he heard a creak coming from the direction of the stairs. Holding his breath and remaining utterly motionless, he listened hard. Another creak made the hair on his scalp rise, and he bit back the whimper growing in his throat.

From his loft room on the third floor, he heard a series of dull thuds, which sounded like they were coming from the first level of the home. Feeling terribly vulnerable, he bit his cheeks so that his teeth would stop chattering in fear, and slid slowly out from under the sheet, wincing when the floor under his feet made a soft squeak. Holding his breath again, he listened. The sounds were still happening downstairs, so apparently whoever was in the house hadn't heard the squeak. He unplugged his cell phone from the charger on the nightstand, then headed for the ensuite bathroom, where he could at least place a locked door between himself and the intruder.

Sitting on the steps that led up to the large jetted tub, Scott pulled his knees up to his chest and turning his phone to silent, texted Echo.

"There's someone in the house—HELP!!! I'm hiding in the bathroom on the 3rd floor."

He waited for a return text, hoping that Echo kept her phone nearby when she went to bed, and wrapped the phone in a washcloth so that even the vibration of an incoming text wouldn't be audible. The teenager's eyes went wide when he heard heavy footsteps thudding on the stairs. Clearly, the wearer of the work boots didn't care a bit whether the scared boy on the third floor knew that they were coming or not.

Scott's blood ran cold as the steps came closer and closer. The phone in his hand buzzed and he nearly dropped it, he was so rattled.

"I'm on my way. Stay in the bathroom!"

He tried to still his breathing, tried to slow down his pounding heart as he heard the heavy tread coming into the bedroom and straight for the bathroom door. He couldn't draw breath and thought his heart would explode when he heard the door handle jiggle, as whoever was on the other side turned it right and left. There was a moment of silence, then a whisper of sound as a slip of paper came swishing under the door. Scott recognized the paper as coming from a pale yellow pad in the kitchen. It had writing on it, but there was no way that he was going to move over to the door and pick it up. He bit down on the end of the washcloth, terrified.

The boots shuffled around outside the door for a moment, then Scott heard a light tapping, as though someone was striking the wood with just a fingernail. He shivered in fear and still didn't move, hoping that Echo would hurry up and arrive, and that she wouldn't be in danger when she got there. More tapping, then a BOOM! as a fist struck the door. Then the footsteps retreated, moving out of the room and down the stairs.

Scott listened for a long time, hearing nothing. Not a sound. No more footsteps, no car doors slamming, nothing. Even the typical Florida cacophony of insects and frogs had ceased, as though all local nature held its breath. Minutes which seemed like hours passed, and he couldn't take it anymore. He had to get out of the bathroom, out of the house. Once he left the bathroom, he'd just keep sprinting until he reached Illinois. He didn't realize that the impulse came from the crazy level of adrenaline coursing through his system.

With a death grip on his phone, he tiptoed to the door, and stood next to it, listening. Still hearing nothing, he slowly turned the tab, unlocking it, without so much as a telltale click. Slowly he turned the knob to the left and opened the door, screeching in terror when he encountered someone right outside. Hitting the flashlight on her cell phone, Echo shushed him, then grabbed him into a firm embrace, which he gladly returned, trembling all over.

"Oh gosh, I'm so sorry. Are you okay?" Echo whispered, standing back and holding him at arm's length to check.

Scott nodded, embarrassed and swiping away the tears that had come unbidden at the sight of a familiar face.

"He left a note," the teenager turned around and pointed to the yellow slip of paper that remained on the bathroom floor where the intruder had placed it.

"Let me see," Echo moved into the bathroom and squatted down to peer at the note without touching it.

"*You can run, but you can't hide,*" she read, with Scott peering over her shoulder.

The young man suddenly went pale and began shaking his head, unconsciously stepping backward, away from the note.

"No, no, no," he whispered, tears springing to his eyes again.

"Oh sweetie, it's okay. We'll figure something out and keep you safe, I promise," she said, standing and moving toward the distraught teenager.

"No, you don't get it," his voice shook with terror.

"What? What is it, Scott?" Echo's eyes grew wide, taking in the depth of his fear.

"That's my mom's handwriting."

CHAPTER TEN

"I hate to say it darlin, but I don't think that all is well with Jeanette," Missy murmured, sifting through the contents of the missing woman's purse.

"What makes you say that?" Kel looked up from his internet search. He'd been doing some poking around, digging up info on Tommy Mancino, the mechanic whose number he'd found in Jeanette's home office.

"Well, for one thing… a woman never leaves home for an extended period of time without taking her purse, and for another… there was an inhaler in her bedside table drawer."

"An inhaler?" the artist was puzzled.

Missy nodded. "So whether she had asthma or allergies, she'd never have left home without that."

"I don't recall that she ever had allergies or asthma," Kel mused.

"Maybe living around all this farmland did it to her," Missy shrugged.

"Maybe."

"What are you finding out?" she motioned to his laptop.

"It's not good," he sighed, tapping on the keyboard. "Apparently Mr. Mancino has had his share of run-ins with the law."

Missy's eyes widened. This was the man that she was supposed to flirt with in order to try to get some information out of him.

"Bad stuff?" she gulped.

"Bad enough," Kel raised his eyebrows and shook his head, eyes glued to the screen.

Before Missy could inquire further, his phone rang, startling both of them, and Echo's picture appeared on the screen.

"Good morning, my love," Kel smiled when he answered. "What?? When?" His face turned to stone. "Is he okay? Are you okay? No, don't worry about it, I'm coming home. I'll be on the next plane out," he glanced at his watch, leaving Missy wondering what was going on.

He asked a few more questions, told his fiancée that he loved her and started gathering his things the minute he hung up the phone.

"Kel, what is it? What happened? Is Echo okay?"

"She's fine, but it seems as though whoever has Jeanette knows where Scott is now, and was sophisticated enough to disarm my alarm system and break into my house."

Missy gasped, her hands going to her throat. "Oh no... Scott?" she whispered.

"Echo says he's fine, and she's not leaving him alone. She'll keep him at her house until I get back, and I'm letting Spencer know what's going on, but I'd prefer it if you don't mention this to Chas," he looked at her pointedly.

"But Kel, if someone broke into your house..."

The artist shook his head. "I just have this strong feeling that bringing the police into this matter would potentially endanger Jeanette and Scott. If we run out of options, I assure you, your brilliant spouse will be the first person that I turn to."

"Okay," she agreed, worried. "Email me those links to the information about the mechanic when you have a moment."

Kel stopped his frenzied packing and stared at her for a moment. "Wait... aren't you going to be flying back to Calgon with me?" he asked.

Missy met his eyes with determination. "You need to go back to Calgon to take care of Scott and your pregnant fiancée... and I need to stay here and figure out what happened to that poor boy's mama," she said, her lower lip trembling for just a moment.

Kel recognized that look, he'd seen it before on the tough little blonde's face. Nothing he could say or do was going to change her mind.

"Chas will eviscerate me if anything happens to you."

"Chas doesn't need to know anything other than that I've decided to stay in this lovely town for a bit longer to enjoy myself and do a bit of exploring."

The artist quirked a skeptical eyebrow. "And you expect him to believe that?"

"He trusts me," her gaze was steady.

"He's sure as heck not going to trust me after this," he muttered.

"Sometimes we have to make sacrifices to do what's right, darlin," was the steady reply.

Kel tried to speak and cleared his throat, overwhelmed at the depth of her friendship and the goodness of her heart. Missy held her arms open and he went into them for a heartfelt hug.

"Thank you," he whispered hoarsely. "If anything happens to you..."

"You hush that crazy talk, and go take care of my best girl," she ordered patting him on the back. "Do you need a ride to the airport?"

"No, I think it's best if we're not seen together, I'll take a shuttle. Are you sure you're up for this?" he asked as she headed for the door with her purse and Jeanette's, along with her notebook.

"You're darn straight I am. Give Echo a squeeze for me," she grinned bravely. And then she was gone.

***

With the links that Kel had provided to her, Missy learned probably more than she had wanted to know about Tommy Mancino. Rhonda the realtor had been correct, he was extremely good-looking, movie-star good-looking in fact. The mechanic was tall and muscular, with curly black hair and soulful chocolate eyes. He'd tried to make a living as a musician, but had apparently supplemented his meager income by engaging in drug trafficking, theft, and various other dangerous-sounding crimes. He'd paid his debt to society, however, and was now a free man, working at Sal's Garage. Well, at least if she had to go talk with the ex-criminal, she'd have something pretty to look at. Whether a hardened playboy like that would give her forty-something self the time of day was another story, and she figured she'd just have to dress the part.

Instead of hitting one of the stylish boutiques downtown, Missy headed for the mall to buy clothing that might help her get some information out of Tommy Mancino. The heat and humidity in central Illinois was nothing compared to Calgon's sultry clime, so, even though it was summer, she bought a snug pair of designer jeans and paired them with an off-the-shoulder turquoise top and matching jute wedges. There was no way in the world that she was going to a car repair shop in shorts or a skirt. She bought a tube of bright pink lipstick and a pair of dangly earrings to complete her ensemble, and when she put everything together in her hotel room, she had to giggle at her reflection, that of a middle-aged Barbie doll. Fortunately, Tommy was in his early fifties, so she hoped the disguise would do the trick.

Putting the address to Sal's Garage into her phone, she made her way toward a shabbier part of town and pulled into the parking lot. She got out of the car and locked it, looking around and trying her best to appear as a helpless female.

"Hey sweetheart, what can I do for ya?" a grizzled mechanic, clearly not Tommy Mancino, popped his head out from under the hood of a well-worn piece of heavy American metal and gave her a lopsided leer after appraising her from head to toe.

"Hi, are you Tommy?" Missy asked sweetly, tilting her head to one side.

"Doll, I'm whoever you need me to be. You got car troubles?"

Missy nodded, batting her kitten-grey eyes in what she hoped was a fetching manner. "I have a friend who knows Tommy and she said that maybe he'd come out and take a look at my car for me."

"Tell ya what, you pull it into that bay over there, and I'll take a look myself," the mechanic gestured with an oily hand.

"Oh, well, it's not this car… it's a different one, and I…" Missy fidgeted, trying to figure out what to say next.

"Hey, Sal! You making time with the lady by pretending to be me again?" Tommy Mancino teased, appearing in the doorway of the shop. There was no mistaking that this had to be the ruggedly handsome man whom Rhonda the realtor had told Kel about. He even had great teeth. He gave Missy a look that was more friendly than leering, which should have put her at ease, but there was something about his demeanor that gave her a slight chill.

"Good afternoon, pretty lady," he flirted. "What can I do to help a damsel in distress this afternoon?" he asked, standing in front of her, hands on hips that were clad in bad boy jeans.

Missy giggled, hoping to make herself sound innocent and not terribly bright. "Well… it's silly, really, but… is there someplace more private that we can talk?" she asked in a voice low enough to make him lean in to hear her.

Sal shook his head and went back to work, accustomed to having women of all ages stop by to try and work their wiles on Tommy. What some women wouldn't do to try and get a discount on getting their car fixed. Mancino studied her for a moment, those chocolate eyes seeming more shrewd than she'd expected, and Missy held her breath, hoping that he wasn't on to her ruse.

"Sure, honey, come on in here," he directed, touching her lightly on the elbow to guide her into the office. "What's your name?"

"Uh... Mindy. Mindy... Baker," Missy lied with a smile, trying not to flinch away from the casual touch on her arm.

"So what can I do for you, Mindy Baker? Coffee?" he asked, pouring himself a cup of what looked like day-old sludge.

"No, I'm good. Thanks. Coffee makes me jittery," she giggled nervously.

"Looks like you've already had some," he observed, raising an eyebrow. Thick muscles flexed beneath tattoos as he stirred cream into his cup of sludge. "What's on your mind?" Suddenly his smile seemed less friendly, his gaze more probing.

Missy's heart raced, and she fought hard to maintain what she hoped was a nonchalant smile.

"Well, I'm a little envious, actually. My friend Jeanie Hammond has a bit of a crush on you, and she hasn't called me for days, so I was kinda thinking that she maybe has… better things to do than talk to her buddy on the phone, but I miss her, and I was hoping maybe you could just tell her to call me?" she blushed, looking down at her hands, then back up at Tommy with her big grey eyes.

His face was impassive and he stared at her for a moment before he spoke.

"You're barking up the wrong tree, lady. It ain't like that with Jeanie and me. She's got a boyfriend. You talk to him?" he challenged, the easygoing smile completely gone.

Missy swallowed hard, but maintained her clueless smile.

"I know she's seeing someone, but she sure talked an awful lot about you," she shrugged, feeling more uncomfortable by the second as Tommy's eyes darkened and narrowed.

"Seems to me like if one of your girlfriends goes missing, the first place you'd look would be with the boyfriend," he said quietly. "The guy's got a cabin down south a couple hours. I would bet that Jeanie's hanging out there, just for a break or something, but who knows? I heard he's got a mean streak. So, you got car problems or what?" he challenged, clearly done talking.

Missy's mind raced as she tried to figure out her next move, feeling like she was missing something.

"Uh... no, I don't have car problems, but I think I may have lost my necklace in Jeanie's car when we went out a couple weeks ago, do you mind if I take a look and try to find it?" she smiled sweetly, somehow keeping her lips from trembling.

"Sorry, I can't let you into another customer's car, that ain't right," Tommy shook his head and crossed his arms over his impressively large chest.

"Oh, it's okay, you don't have to let me in," she smiled. "I have a key."

"You have a key," he repeated, staring at her.

"Yup," she moved toward the door.

"Knock yourself out then," he muttered, opening the office door to let her out.

Well, that certainly hadn't gone as well as she'd expected, but at least now Missy had access to the car and hoped to find some sort of clue. She searched the interior high and low, under seats, in the glove compartment, in the side pockets of the doors, the center console, and the pocket on the back of the front seats, then popped the trunk to have a look back there. She was bent over at the waist, using her phone as a flashlight, when Tommy's voice startled her, making her bolt upright, banging her head on the trunk. She winced and rubbed at the sore spot.

"You thinking you lost your necklace back here?" he drawled, eyebrows raised.

"It was a long shot, but I did help her unload groceries, so it was possible," Missy turned on the charm. Apparently Tommy was no longer buying it.

"You done here? Sal and I got work to do before we close up for the day."

"Oh! Sure, yes, I'm sorry. I didn't mean to be a bother. Thanks for letting me take a look," she smiled, turning and heading for her rental car, trying not to walk conspicuously fast.

Tommy turned away and sneezed three times in rapid succession.

"Bless you," Missy said automatically, looking at him and noticing his red, bloodshot eyes for the first time. "Poor thing, do you have a cold?"

"Nahhh... allergies. This time of year sucks for me because of the harvesting starting."

"Aww... that's too bad," she sympathized, a red flag going up in her mind. Lost in thought, she turned again to go.

106

"Nice accent. Where you from, Mindy?" he called after her.

Kicking herself for not trying harder to conceal her Louisiana drawl, she turned back briefly.

"Tennessee," she replied, continuing on her way. "You can take the girl out of the South, but you can't take the South out of the girl."

He nodded, eyeing her speculatively. "Tennessee, huh?" he muttered.

She was too far away to hear him.

CHAPTER ELEVEN

Kel rushed into Echo's cozy cottage, found Scott, and hugged him tight.

"I'm so sorry that happened to you," he said, searching the teenager's eyes.

"I'm okay," the youth shrugged, trying to smile. "Echo is a pretty good rescuer."

The artist moved to his fiancée and took her gently into his arms.

"My precious love, why on earth didn't you call the police? I don't know what I would've done if something had happened to you," he closed his eyes and kissed her hair, while Scott occupied himself with checking the wax levels in the dipping vats.

"I couldn't call the police," she whispered. "Remember? Involving them might mean that Jeanette could get hurt."

Kel held his bride-to-be at arm's length and gazed into her eyes for a moment. He'd never known it was possible to love someone so much.

"You put your life in danger in order to protect a woman you've never met. Your fiancé's ex-girlfriend that you've never met," his eyes were filled with admiration.

"She's the mother of your son, and your son is a part of you… I can't turn my back on that. Never," she shook her head, placing her palm on his cheek.

"You're an amazing woman."

They were both a bit startled when they heard Chas's voice coming from the front hall.

"Echo? You home?" the detective called out.

Echo looked at Kel wide-eyed.

"I'll be out in a second," she replied, then turned back to her fiancé. "Why is he here?" she whispered. "Did Missy tell him what's going on?"

The artist sighed. "I certainly hope not. She's still in Illinois."

"Good afternoon, Kel," Chas greeted the artist. "I wasn't aware that you had returned to Calgon, but it looks like my lovely wife must have done an incredibly good job of convincing you not to get involved," he commented dryly.

The artist met his gaze, and simply stared for a moment, formulating a response.

"Well, I'm obviously not a detective," he said finally.

"That never really stopped you before," Chas observed. "Kel... you and I both know that my Missy sometimes gets herself involved with situations that might be hazardous to her health. I'd hate to think that you'd left her alone in another state under those kinds of circumstances," the detective gave him a pointed look.

"I care very deeply for your dear wife. If I had suspected that she might be putting herself in harm's way, I would not have felt comfortable leaving her there."

"Just so we're on the same page in that regard."

"Indeed," Kel nodded.

Chas leaned against the foyer wall, looking from Echo to Kel and back again.

"We had a citizen's report come in from one of your neighbors last night."

"Oh?" Kel said, as he and Echo exchanged a look.

The detective nodded.

"A sweet little old neighbor lady was awake and feeding her cats when she heard a lot of banging coming from your place. Said she saw a young man jump your fence and run shortly after, then saw Echo pull your car into the driveway. Wanna tell me what that was all about?"

Echo blinked, then swallowed and spoke.

"Kel's son, Scott, was housesitting while Kel was in Illinois, and he was woken up by a bunch of strange sounds coming from the downstairs, so doing the smart thing, he ran into the bathroom, locked the door and texted me," she explained.

"That must have been scary," Chas mused.

"Terrifying," Echo nodded.

"Then why, when you got that text, did you not call 911, or me, for that matter?"

Echo's mouth gaped a bit as she tried to come up with an appropriate response.

"I... I don't... I just... was so upset, that I... wasn't thinking clearly. I just wanted to get to Scott and make sure that he was safe. I didn't even think about who might be in the house or why," she said shakily.

"Understandable," Chas looked at her carefully. "Was anything damaged or missing?"

"No, not that I could tell," Kel replied, so that Echo wouldn't have to.

"What was the condition of the house when you arrived?" the detective turned back to Echo.

"All the doors on the lower level were open, all the drawers and cabinets in the kitchen were open, and Kel's desk in the study had been gone through," she answered, not mentioning the note that had been slipped under the bathroom door.

"Sounds like whoever it was, was looking for something. Any idea what that might be?" Chas asked Kel.

"Not a clue," the artist shook his head.

"What about the alarm system? Was it set and operational?"

"I set it when I left after we watched a movie," Echo nodded. "It seemed to work just fine."

Chas raised his eyebrows. "Mind if I drop by and take a look around? Might see something that you two missed in all the excitement."

"That'd be great," Kel replied, shaking the detective's hand.

"I can meet you at Betty's for lunch and we can swing by your place after," Chas suggested.

"Sounds good."

"Nice seeing you Echo," the detective gave her a hug and went on his way.

"You too," she murmured.

She and Kel exchanged a worried glance.

"It can't hurt to let him have a look, right?" she whispered.

Kel shrugged. "If he finds something important, we'll just have to explain what's going on and try to get him to not do anything in an official capacity."

"Easier said than done," Echo bit her lip.

"Indeed."

***

Chas was nearly finished with his examination of Kel's massive home, when something on top of a stack of papers caught his eye.

"Kel, what does your housekeeper look like?" he asked, slipping a handful of plastic evidence bags out of his pocket.

"Linda is about five feet tall, on the thin side, bright red hair, brown eyes… why?"

"So it would be safe to assume that this didn't come from her," the detective observed, holding up a curly black hair with tweezers.

"I'd say so," Kel agreed, his stomach churning a bit.

"And this pen is on top of everything, so I'm going to hope that the perpetrator picked it up at some point," Chas continued, slipping the pen into another bag. "And it looks like this legal pad may have been used too." He took the yellow pad of paper and put it into yet another evidence bag. "I recovered another black hair outside the bathroom door," he patted his pocket, then turned to address his friend very frankly.

"Look, Kel, you and I both know that this incident could be connected to your son's missing mother. Let me slip some things through the lab. I have some techs who owe me favors. It can't hurt to at least try to track down who did this, because there's someone out there who may pose a danger to you, Echo, or Scott. Don't you want to find out who it is?" the detective asked reasonably.

"Of course," Kel let out a breath, actually glad that Chas would be pitching in to help. "I'm sorry, I just haven't even been able to think straight lately. With the baby, and Scott and Jeanette, and Echo not feeling well…" he shook his head.

"I hear you my friend, and I'm here to help," Chas snapped off his rubber gloves and gave the artist's shoulder a reassuring squeeze.

CHAPTER TWELVE

Missy tossed her giant earrings on the counter, squirmed out of the tight jeans and top and into gym shorts and a t-shirt, then wiped the hot pink lipstick from her mouth with a tissue. She hadn't found any clues; she hadn't really had a substantial conversation with Tommy Mancino, who, despite his good looks seemed rather scary; and she hadn't learned anything new, other than Stanton Vincenzo had an alleged mean streak.

Tommy Mancino had been to prison, but when they'd looked at his activities since his release, he'd seemed like a model citizen, not having even so much as a parking ticket. Stanton Vincenzo had seemed to Kel like a genuinely nice guy who was a little bit too smooth for comfort, and none of what either one of them had found out pointed to how or why Jeanette Hammond had disappeared. A couple of things were popping up in Missy's brain as red flags though… she had seen allergy drugs in Jeanette's drawer, and Kel had said that as far as he knew, Jeanette didn't have allergies. When she talked to Tommy Mancino, he'd said that his allergies were driving him crazy, yet Tommy pretended that he didn't have a relationship of any substance with Jeanie. Were the allergy meds Tommy's? Was he trying to conceal the fact that he and Jeanette were more involved than he was admitting?

Then there was the matter of the cabin belonging to Stanton Vincenzo that Tommy had mentioned. Maybe Missy should go see Stanton herself. Maybe she could get answers out of the smooth-talking man that Kel hadn't. Maybe she'd have to wear the tight jeans and jute heels one more time. No, when she really thought about it, trying to act like someone else really hadn't turned out that well, so when she went to visit Stanton Vincenzo, she vowed to be much more true to who she really was, but she'd try better to hide her southern accent.

Wrung out after her encounter with Tommy Mancino, Missy flopped back on the bed and nearly jumped out of her skin when she heard a banging on the door across the hall that used to be Kel's room.

"Champaign County Sheriff's Department, open up!" a stern voice commanded, only to be met with silence.

Missy covered her mouth with her hands, heart pounding. The voice tried a couple more times before instructing the hotel manager to open the door with a room key. She was thankful that the maid had cleaned the room shortly after Kel left, so hopefully there would be no traces of him left in the cool, sophisticated space. She held her breath, hoping against hope that no one had yet made the connection between her and Kel, and sagged into a chair when the police finally left, after inspecting the room.

"Yeah, he's long gone," she heard one of the officers remark, and hoped that Kel wasn't now a suspect of some sort.

Missy knew that she had to make progress and quickly. Every day that passed was another chance for something awful to happen to Jeanette Hammond, and she couldn't stomach the thought of a nice young man like Scott losing his mother. She'd go see Stanton Vincenzo in the morning, and in the meantime, she'd search property records trying to locate his cabin. It would be like looking for a needle in a haystack, but it was better than doing nothing. She would also run more searches on Tommy Mancino, who seemed like a potentially dangerous man.

Missy's eyes were blurred with lack of sleep, and she wiped at them with the back of her hand, suddenly feeling very much awake after a few hours of searching for Vincenzo's cabin. She'd come across a picture of Stanton and four of his friends, standing in front of a gorgeous log-cabin type home. The caption on the photo said "Kaufman Lake, 2014." After finding the photo, she'd done a search for property records in Kaufman Lake, Illinois, using Stanton's name, and had stumbled across the deed to the property. It turned out that the "cabin" was a luxury lakefront home with its own dock.

She jotted down the address, and considered the possibility of checking out the home after speaking with Stanton in the morning.

***

Missy took one last look in the mirror before heading out to Stanton Vincenzo's office. She'd elected to wear comfortable capris and an age-appropriate sleeveless sweater, with white patent leather kitten-heeled mules, and modest pearl earrings, capping off her look with a simple messy bun, leaving stray tendrils of hair trailing along her face and neck. She was glad that the morning cool hadn't yet given way to the hot and humid day that the weatherman on the news last night had predicted. She took a deep breath, started the car, and headed toward Vincenzo's office.

Telling the receptionist that she was there to see Mr. Vincenzo on a personal matter, Missy sat in the waiting room, playing a word game on her phone to calm her nerves.

"Mindy Baker?" the accountant asked, emerging from the inner sanctum. "Come with me please, young lady," he gestured for her to enter ahead of him, then instructed her where to turn for his office. Once they were seated, he in his leather executive chair, she in a simple club chair across from him, he folded his hands on the desk and smiled at her expectantly.

"How may I assist you today?" he asked pleasantly.

"Actually, I came here today because I'm worried about a friend of mine, and I'm hoping that you might be able to help."

"Is your friend in need of an accountant?" the smile didn't falter.

"No, Mr. Vincenzo, my friend is Jeanette Hammond. Do you happen to know where she might be? I haven't seen or heard from her in over two weeks, and I'm worried about her. It's just not like her to disappear like that, without a word to anyone."

Stanton Vincenzo's face drooped, and he shook his head.

"I'll tell you what, Mindy, I'm worried about her too. You're not the only one who's asking around about her. Seems like she just disappeared, but then on the other hand, if you know her well, you know that sometimes she just likes to get away from it all and not talk to nobody, you know what I'm saying?"

"Sure, yes," Missy nodded, hoping that was the case. "But if she didn't even tell you where she was going... isn't that a little strange?"

"Well, it ain't like we was married or something," Stanton chuckled, his Chicago accent profound, then he sobered. "In fact, I wonder if any of this has to do with the fact that she got mixed up with that ex-con mechanic, Mancino," he said in a low voice, giving her a knowing look.

"Were they dating?" Missy asked, trying to sound sympathetic rather than nosy.

Vincenzo shrugged. "Call it what you will... word has it that he spent some nights at her place. That's all I'm saying."

"Is he... dangerous?" she gulped, not faking. She'd just spent time with that man.

"Who knows?" he spread his hands, palms up in a gesture of frustrated ignorance. "All I know is that she starts seeing an ex-con, and then she up and disappears. You do the math, honey. I ain't trying to scare you, I'm just being real, ya know?"

"Could there maybe be other friends that she might have gone to stay with?" Missy thought aloud, realizing her mistake as the words left her mouth.

Stanton's eyes tightened just a fraction at the corners and he paused a moment, leaning back in his chair and cocking his head to one side to study her.

"Well, as her friend, you'd know more about that than I would, am I right?" he challenged, raising his eyebrows.

"Yes, of course. I just thought maybe... well, whatever. It doesn't matter now. I'm sorry to have wasted your time," Missy practically leapt from her chair and backed toward the door.

"Oh, Miss Baker?" Vincenzo said slowly, with a smile that seemed almost smug.

"Yes?" Missy answered breathlessly.

"You'll want to be careful about digging into other people's private affairs... there are some nasty folks out there. Very nasty folks," he warned, his eyes like daggers.

Missy stared at him, tempted to make a cutting retort, but not wanting to make him entirely suspicious.

"Yes, Mr. Vincenzo," she finally replied, staring him down. "Apparently there are."

***

Missy drove away from the accounting firm more determined than ever to find the cabin and hopefully get to the bottom of Jeanette's disappearance. She'd been terribly suspicious of Tommy Mancino, but now she was equally suspicious of Stanton Vincenzo. She'd found addresses for both men, and planned to drive by their houses just out of curiosity, while they were both safely at work.

Tommy Mancino lived in a very middle-class condo complex on the south side of Champaign, which featured a small pond and an even smaller swimming pool that seemed to be the center of the social scene for the complex. He had a balcony overlooking the dumpsters and the pool, and there were pool towels hung up to dry on the backs of vinyl patio chairs. There were two women who looked to be in their thirties, sunning themselves in bikinis on loungers by the pool, so Missy walked over to have a friendly conversation and see what she could learn.

"Hey ladies! Beautiful day, isn't it?" she grinned, shading her eyes with her hand. She'd tucked her shiny blonde ponytail up inside a baseball cap, and had worn large sunglasses, so it was difficult to see what she looked like.

"Mmhmm..." one of them agreed. Both of them looked at her curiously.

"I'm a friend of Tommy's. Have you seen him around?"

"I wish," one of them sighed dramatically, and they both chuckled. "Nahh... he doesn't usually come to the pool until after his evening run... around seven."

"You his girlfriend or something?" the other suntanned resident asked.

Missy laughed. "Definitely not. I'm married."

"That never stopped Tommy before," the pair laughed again.

"I just thought maybe he'd know where one of my friends might be. They were kind of seeing each other."

One of the ladies sat up, stretching. "Well, if you know anything about Tommy, you know that he never brings any of his 'girls' home. I haven't seen a woman at his place since he moved in, and I live directly across from him, so I'd know. You're not going to find your friend here, honey," she finished and lay back down, closing her eyes and basking in the sun.

Missy was baffled. "Okay, thanks anyway," she waved and went on her way.

Her next stop was Stanton Vincenzo's house, across town to the west. The accountant lived in the same golf course community as Jeanette, but in the much more expensive end of it, where buying a membership to the exclusive country club was a requirement for home ownership. One end of the desirable neighborhood was gated, and Missy hoped that Stanton's house was in the end that wasn't. Her GPS led her past the stately brick homes belonging to Champaign's best and brightest, and she came to a stop in front of Vincenzo's house, her mouth dropping open in amazement.

From the white pillars out front, to the topiaries by the massive mahogany double doors, and the sparkling swimming pool out back, Stanton's house was stunning. A circular drive and artfully placed landscaping graced the front of the palatial home, and Missy wondered just how on earth a middle-aged accountant in a small firm in central Illinois had managed to afford it. She'd have to see if perhaps Stanton came from a wealthy family. Had that been part of what had made him attractive to Jeanette? She quickly brushed such thoughts from her mind, determined not to try and second guess the thoughts and motives of a missing woman.

An idea came to Missy on her way back to the hotel. One way to find out more about Tommy Mancino, who actually seemed to be the more suspicious of the two men that she was investigating, would be to follow him. There were nifty little cul-de-sacs in the condo complex that would allow her to find a vantage point where she could watch Mancino's condo without being detected, then follow him whenever he left. Filled with a new sense of determination and purpose, Missy went back to her room, had some lunch, and planned her evening. She'd follow Tommy tonight, hoping that somehow he might lead her to Jeanette, and tomorrow, early, she'd go find Stanton's cabin.

CHAPTER THIRTEEN

Detective Chas Beckett opened his email and found that the reports he'd requested from his friend at the lab had come in. There were roots on the hairs that he'd recovered from Kel's house after it had been invaded, and there was enough DNA to have made a match to a known criminal in the database. There was also a partial print that was a match to the same person.

His throat suddenly dry, Chas picked up the phone and called Kel.

"How well do you now know Jeanette?" he asked without preamble when the artist answered.

"Not very, why?" Kel was alarmed at the detective's tone.

"I was able to get a match for the hair and fingerprints that were found at your house. They belong to a small-time hood named Ricky 'The Raccoon' Raguso, who keeps very bad company," Chas informed his friend.

"How bad?"

"He's been linked to organized crime."

"The mob?" there was a chord of fear in Kel's voice.

"The mob. I've gotta get Missy out of there," Chas's jaw clenched.

"What can I do to help?"

"Take Scott and Echo and get out of here. What happened at your house was meant to send a message of some sort. Until we know for sure what that message is, we can't assume that you or any member of your family is safe. You'll probably want to warn Jeanette's parents to be extra cautious too, but whatever you do, get out of town as fast as you can. I'll let you know when I have Missy back home, safe and sound."

Without giving Kel time to even reply, Chas hung up the phone and immediately dialed his wife's number.

***

Despite dealing with pregnancy-induced fatigue and the stress of wondering what was happening with Scott and his mother, Echo had resolved that she would work as hard as she could for as long as she could before the baby came. There were employees to hire and training to complete so that Joyce Rutledge, her ever-so-capable manager wouldn't be overwhelmed with trying to run a bookstore and adjoining candle shop at the same time by herself. Joyce was a superwoman when it came to working hard and working smart, but even she had limits and Echo didn't want to put her in a bad position; therefore, she planned to be at work as much as possible over the course of the next few months, to help her prepare.

The two ladies had been accepting applications and conducting interviews, and would continue to do so until the perfect candidates were found.

"You look tired, Miss Echo," Joyce observed, stuffing bundles of bills into a bank bag to deposit on her way home.

"I'm just dragging, Joyce. I've had plenty of vitamin B-12, and I'm making sure that I get enough protein, now that I can actually eat without throwing everything up an hour later, but I just get so tired by the end of the day," Echo sighed, stirring a cup of tea.

"That's not unusual," Joyce smiled. "I think every mama-to-be feels that way a good part of the time. You just have to know when your body is telling you to sit down and put your feet up," she cautioned.

"Right now I feel like lying down and going to sleep," Echo smiled faintly.

"I can finish up here if you want to go ahead and take off," the big-hearted young woman offered.

"No, Joyce, I can…" she began, only to be interrupted by Kel bursting into the shop, looking mussed and sweaty, something she'd never seen before, at least not during daylight hours.

"Sweetheart, you need to come with me," he said urgently.

"I… uh…" Echo was baffled. She'd never seen her fiancé wild-eyed and stressed like this.

"You go on, Miss Echo. I got this," Joyce piped up, assessing Kel and recognizing a bad situation when she saw one.

"Thank you, Joyce. Your pay will be double for the next few days," Kel promised, dragging his fiancée from the store as fast as her feet would take her.

"Goodness, Kel, what's going on?" she demanded, getting into his car, where Scott was waiting.

"I'll tell you more later. For now, we're headed to the airport," he replied, gunning the engine and cutting his eyes toward where Scott sat wide-eyed in the back seat.

***

Missy was in the shower when Chas's call came in, so she never heard her phone ringing. When she turned the phone to silent and threw it in her purse, she was already on her way out the door to go keep watch at Tommy Mancino's condo, so she didn't notice that her husband had left a message. She didn't want to take a chance that a text tone or game notification might sound, alerting the intense man to her presence. She slid the little powder-blue car into a parking spot where she could see Tommy's condo without him seeing her, and wished that the rental company had given her a less conspicuously colored vehicle. Grey, white, and black vehicles were a dime a dozen, but her powder-blue, late-model compact stood out like a petunia among sunflowers.

She waited patiently for the sun to set, watched Tommy arrive back from his run, go upstairs to his condo, ostensibly to shower, then come down and swim laps in the pool while a gaggle of mostly female residents sat back, enjoying the spectacle of the powerfully built man cutting his way through the water. After his swim, he said a few words to some of the spectators, toweled off, and went back inside, emerging a few minutes later fully dressed. Tommy got into his primer-grey, not completely restored GTO, and headed through the neighborhood, winding his way around roads that were clearly familiar to him and nearly losing Missy several times. She didn't follow too closely, not wanting him to notice her, but she stayed with him until he pulled into a parking lot at a park.

She found a spot on the street to park where she could still watch him but he probably wouldn't see her. Her heart leapt to her throat, and she had to hold back a gasp when she saw him open his trunk and pull out a long black duffel bag. Guns? He was bringing guns to a public park?? Hands shaking, she reached for her phone, not taking her eyes off of Tommy Mancino as he headed directly toward a group of ragtag boys. There were only two other adults present, were they his target... or were the children? Glancing down at her phone, Missy realized that her hands were shaking too hard to dial 911, so she set the phone down on her leg and looked up just as Mancino unzipped the bag.

"No, no... oh, no," she murmured, her hand going to her throat in horror.

He reached into the bag, locked eyes with one of the boys in front of him as he drew out... an aluminum baseball bat. There were several in the bag, and he handed them all out in preparation for batting practice. Missy nearly fainted with relief and willed her heart to stop pounding before it leapt from her chest. She leaned her head back and closed her eyes, trying to take deep breaths, only to be startled again by a light tapping on her window. Opening her eyes in a flash, she nearly jumped out of her seat when she saw Tommy Mancino crouched next to the car, grinning. He made a motion for her to roll down the window, and when she shook her head no, he made it again, rolling his eyes a bit.

Missy lowered the window about halfway.

"May I help you?" she said shakily.

"I told you, lady, you're barking up the wrong tree," Mancino said affably. "If you wanna find your friend, I'd be taking a hard look at the boyfriend. Might wanna find a different car first though, Sherlock. And just be advised… these people don't mess around. Vincenzo would eat you for lunch without a second thought."

With that, he sauntered off, heading back to teach nine-year-olds how to hit a curve ball.

***

Chas Beckett was worried sick. His wife wasn't picking up her phone, and wasn't returning his calls. If she didn't answer him before bed tonight, he'd be on a plane to Illinois first thing in the morning.

***

Missy was flat-out disgusted with how ineffective she'd been thus far. She kept arousing distrust in her suspects and hadn't yet gotten any vital information as to where Jeanette Hammond might be and why. She felt as if she had failed poor Scott, and determined to do more. She went back to her hotel after sticking around to talk to the other coaches. Once Mancino had gone, she'd found out that Tommy spent every Tuesday, Friday, and Saturday coaching baseball, which made it very unlikely that he was involved with Jeanette's disappearance, since she was last seen on a Friday.

135

Exhausted, she plugged her phone into the charger without even looking at it, still berating herself for being "caught" so easily in the act of following Tommy Mancino. Tomorrow was another day, and she'd be heading to southern Illinois, to check out Stanton Vincenzo's lake house.

***

Chas let himself into his wife's room, only to find that she was gone. There were no signs of struggle, and nothing that gave him any indication of where she might be. He searched the room thoroughly and found only two things, the name of a local accounting firm, and directions to a place called Kaufman Lake. He'd begin with the accounting firm, then follow the directions to Kaufman Lake if he didn't hear from Missy in the meantime.

***

Missy slowed her little rental car to a halt when her GPS announced that she had arrived at Vincenzo's lake house. She sat with the engine running, staring at the metal gate which was currently barring access to the property, pondering what her best move might be. There was no room on either side of the gate to bypass it because of heavy vegetation, and the gate itself was chained and padlocked shut. She wasn't a vandal, and didn't have the means to cut the chain anyway, so she was stymied for a bit. Her determination overrode her lack of resources, however, and she swiveled in her seat, looking for a suitable place to pull off the road.

Spotting a break in the trees a few yards ahead, Missy pulled the rental car off into a patch of tall grass and weeds, got out, and locked it. If she couldn't drive down the private road which led to the lake house, she'd walk it. Glancing down at her cell phone to silence it, she noted that the little "No Service Available" icon had appeared on her screen, but she switched the phone over to silent just in case, rather than taking the chance that it might chime or buzz at precisely the wrong time if she happened to wander into an area where it picked up a signal again. Thankful that she had worn comfy jeans, running shoes, and a close-fitting tee shirt, she climbed the metal pole gate, swung her leg over, and dropped onto the other side of it without much effort at all.

Missy didn't bother trying to hide the fact that she was approaching the house, walking right down the middle of the private road, because the house was apparently quite a distance from the gate. She hadn't caught sight of it even after having walked for at least ten minutes. Sweat trailed a path down her spine, ending at her jeans; and pesky insects buzzed around her, seeming to stick to her skin when they made contact. She pressed on, knowing that the house would be there eventually, and thinking that she might just go wading in the lake for relief after she checked out the house.

When she caught a glimpse of the stunning contemporary home made of glass and wood and boasting attractive angles everywhere, she slipped into the trees at the side of the road, making her way more carefully toward the expensive structure. There weren't any cars in the drive, so when she neared the lawn, first looking in every direction at least twice, she stepped out of the cover of the trees and approached the house. Feeling more than vulnerable, she walked right up to the front door and rang the bell, then knocked. If anyone answered, she'd make a bogus claim of car trouble and ask to use the phone so that she could pretend to call for assistance. If no one was home, which she really hoped, she'd be able to look around for clues to see if it looked like perhaps Jeanette was being held here.

When there was no initial response, she rang again, calling out, "Anybody home?" Silence greeted her inquiry, for which she was profoundly grateful, so she moved to her left to peer into the living room windows. Vertical blinds obscured her view, but she saw enough to know that the main house was dark inside. Thinking that the more logical place to hold someone captive would be in a basement or outbuilding, she went around to the back of the house, where a walk-out basement led to a trail that meandered toward the lake. When she stepped onto the back deck by the french doors which led out of the basement, she heard a scrabbling sound above her. Heart pounding, she dashed for cover behind a stand of ornamental grass.

Crouching low, she circled around behind the grass, looking for the source of the sound that she'd heard. Relief flooded through her, and she actually laughed aloud when she saw a chipmunk family on the deck that had been directly above her. Glad that the sound hadn't been an indication of something sinister, she stood up straight, and felt something brush against her foot. Instinctively she flinched and nearly fainted on the spot when she looked down and saw the beady eyes and flickering tongue of a snake that had been coiled up in front of the clump of grass. Shrieking, she took off in a full sprint toward the house, not stopping until she was snugged up against the basement door, looking frantically around her feet to see if any more reptiles lurked. As scared as she was of humans with evil intentions, she'd rather face a psychopath than a snake any day.

Missy sagged against the french doors of the walk-out basement, catching her breath and trying to slow her heartbeat. The interior of the basement was dark, just as the living room had been, and she was frustrated that, no matter where she turned, she seemed to run into nothing but a series of dead ends. The silence of the empty luxury home gave her chills, and she wanted nothing more than to run far away from Kaufman Lake, never to return, but she couldn't shake the feeling that she was missing something. Maybe the answer was closer to the lake. After her reptilian encounter, she was more than reluctant to follow the trail from the house to the lake, but her curiosity would not be denied, so after peeking in a few more windows, she trudged down the slate and gravel path toward the lake, her eyes constantly scanning for cold-blooded slitherers.

A large, sleek boat was docked in a peaceful cove, and Missy once again took refuge in the trees to approach the area, this time being much more aware of where she stepped. Peering carefully around the trunk of a massive maple, she didn't see any signs of human occupation, so she made her way to the dock. The sunlight sparkled on the water, and in any other circumstances she would've enjoyed the spectacular view tremendously, but in this moment, for this purpose, her focus was on the large, powerful boat and any secrets that it might contain.

Water lapped against the side of the boat and the dock, and fish swam in and out of the shadows as Missy gingerly stepped aboard the pristine white vessel.

"Hello?" she called out shakily, again planning to use the car trouble story if she had to.

She glanced around the patio area of the boat, seeing only a bottle of suntan lotion in a cup holder, and a towel spread over one of the bench seats. Moving toward the captain's chairs up front, she noticed that the keys were in the ignition, which she found odd. She knocked on the door which led below deck to the tiny galley kitchen and bathroom, then opened it and found nothing that seemed even remotely connected to Jeanette Hammond or a kidnapping. Frustrated that she had wasted an entire day driving down here, only to find nothing, she stepped back onto the dock, shoulders slumped in defeat. It was then that she heard voices, male voices, coming from the direction of the lake house.

Heart in her throat, Missy sprinted for the line of trees as fast as her feet would carry her, making it to cover just as two casually dressed men came into view. She recognized them as associates of Stanton Vincenzo from some photos she'd seen, but she didn't know who they were. The men scanned the area around them carefully as they made their way toward the dock, as Missy crouched down behind a thick wall of bushes, barely daring to breathe.

"You see anything?" one asked, still staring into the trees.

"No, you?"

"Nothin. Let's check out the boat."

While one of the men frowned and went down to the edge of the water, looking carefully in every direction, the other trotted down the dock and peered into the boat.

"Yo, Joey... come take a look at this," he directed.

Joey jogged over to the dock, hopped up onto it and looked where the other man was pointing. Missy was close enough to hear their conversation, and fervently hoped that they couldn't hear her heart thumping.

"Footprint?"

"Looks like it."

"Kinda small," Joey observed.

"Like a chick," the man sounded baffled.

"So who is she, where is she, and why is she here?" Joey mused in a voice that sounded the tiniest bit sinister.

"We need guys down here to search. That rental car we saw has to belong to whoever's hanging around here, so we need to get between here and that car so we can 'detain' the chick and find out what she's about."

"I'll get back to cell range and make some calls," Joey nodded. "You don't supposed it's Vincenzo's broad, do ya?"

"Nah, Vinnie hasn't heard from her in weeks. Said she was messin' around with Mancino after he got outta the joint."

"She didn't seem like Tommy's type."

"Nope. I guess there's just no tellin what a broad will do, ya know?"

"Guess not," Joey shrugged. "I'm headed out. If you find her, bring her to town."

"With pleasure," the other man chuckled.

Joey ran back up the trail toward the house and the other man headed for the stand of trees where Missy was hiding. She was terrified and froze, not knowing what to do, as the man moved closer and closer.

Suddenly, a shadow darted in behind the man, tackling him and taking him down, with an MMA-style choke hold. When the man had been subdued, his assailant stood up.

"Missy?" he called in a low voice that she recognized instantly, and tears of relief sprung to her eyes.

"Chas!" she replied, standing up and heading toward her beloved husband.

"Do you have any idea the kind of danger that you were in?" he mumbled into her hair as he held her tightly to his chest.

"How on earth did you find me here?" she asked, her voice muffled by the front of his shirt.

"We'll talk about all of that later," he said urgently, releasing her. "For right now, we've gotta get you out of here. I found a way to get through the woods and back to your car without having to take the road, but we have to be fast. They realize that someone is here, so we don't have a second to lose," the detective began propelling her back toward the gate, through the woods.

"Who knows we're here?" Missy whispered, dodging limbs and stepping over bushes.

"You really don't want to know," was the grim reply.

CHAPTER FOURTEEN

"Well, if it isn't my favorite Marine," Joyce Rutledge looked up with delight when Spencer Bengal entered the candle shop.

"Hey, Joyce, how's life?" he asked, trying to smile.

Spencer had precious few reasons to smile these days. His girlfriend Izzy had left him without looking back. She wouldn't even answer his texts. He knew he would have to fulfill an obligation to his government that he'd successfully deferred for quite some time in order to protect Chas Beckett, so he would now have to entrust Chas and Missy's safety to another operative. He also knew that chances were better than average that he wouldn't return from his next mission. He had no idea what Steve Arnold, the dark ops watchdog, had in store for him, but knowing Steve, the likelihood was that whatever the mission, he wouldn't return from it in one piece, or at all.

"I'm all right, but what's up with your gloomy handsome face?" Joyce saw right through his sad attempt at a smile.

"Just a lot on my mind right now," he shrugged, avoiding her eyes.

"Mmmhmm…" was the skeptical reply. "Well what brings you to my paradise on earth?" she rested her elbows on the counter and smiled up at him.

"Echo asked me to check in with you occasionally and make sure that you're okay. She said you could just close down for a while if it was too much for you to handle."

"Pshh… too much for Joyce Rutledge to handle? Honey, I don't think so. I'm doing just fine, thank you very much," she grinned. "Now you, on the other hand, look like a man who could use some chocolate cake."

That made him crack a slight smile. "I don't usually indulge."

"Clearly," Joyce replied, deliberately eyeing his abs. "But, Mr. Tall-Dark-and-Healthy, sometimes you just gotta have yourself some good old-fashioned comfort food. Mark my words," she nodded sagely. "I happen to have a slice of devil's food with fudge frosting at home with your name on it," she tempted, raising an eyebrow.

"You do know that I'm spending all day in a cupcake shop right now, right?" he asked.

"Mmmhmmm… and as awesome as Ms. Beckett's cupcakes are, you haven't lived until you've had a piece of Joyce's Sour Cream Chocolate Cake," she challenged, folding her arms.

"I'll think about it," Spencer nodded with a smile.

"Well don't strain yourself, honey, it's an easy decision," she teased, picking up her phone from under the counter. "What's your number, sourpuss? I'm gonna text you later and bug you 'til you wise up and come eat some cake so you'll feel better," she looked at him expectantly.

Knowing when he'd been beaten, Spencer gave her his number.

"Is there anything you need?" he asked, on his way out.

"A dinner companion," she looked at him pointedly, and he chuckled at her brash approach.

"That could happen," he nodded.

"Two words, Spencer... barbecued ribs. You just let that marinate for a little bit, cuz I'm gonna text you later."

"I'll look forward to it," he grinned, giving her a wave on his way out the door.

"Mmm, mmm, mmm, that boy is delicious," she pursed her lips, watching him go.

***

Izzy Gilmore was deeply engrossed in writing her latest horror novel, a light little piece about a monstrous serial killer who liked to torment his victims for months prior to capturing, torturing and killing them. She'd just described a gruesome scene, involving a dentist's drill and a straightjacket, when her doorbell rang, startling her.

The phenomenally successful author lived in a cute little pink and white cottage in Calgon that, while located in a typical upper-middle-class neighborhood, was set back far enough from the street to ensure her privacy; therefore, she was surprised to hear her doorbell ring out of the blue. Except for Missy, Echo, and until now, Spencer, Izzy had no friends in town and she liked it that way. Solicitors and surveyors tended to just skip past her house rather than wind their way through the delightful landscaping, past the white picket fence gate, and up the driveway. The sleepy little beachside town allowed her to hide from her fans and publisher and write in peace.

Annoyed at the interruption, Izzy sighed and went to the door, half expecting to see Missy or Echo, despite the fact that both women always called or texted before coming over. When she peered through the peephole, she saw a gleaming red sports car parked at the curb and a tall man with thinning brown hair on her doorstep.

"Yes?" she opened the door a few inches, frowning at the man on the other side.

"Hi Izzy," the man grinned. "I'm Steve Arnold, and I'd like to speak with you for a moment about a Marine named Spencer Bengal, if I may."

Alarm bells went off in Izzy's mind. Very few people knew who Spencer was, and even fewer knew that he lived in Calgon and had dated her. He'd told her that there were dangerous people who were looking for him, and for all she knew, this man, who looked like a professional golfer, might be one of them.

"I'm sorry, I have no idea who you're talking about," she said, as sweetly as she could manage, and moved to shut the door.

Steve had his foot in between the door and the jamb in a flash and put his hand against the thick wood slab to arrest its progress as well.

"I must not have made myself clear, Miss Gilmore," he said with the same smile that didn't even come close to reaching his eyes. "I'm here in the interest of national security and I need to speak with you about Spencer Bengal."

"Get your foot out of the way, and get off of my property before I start screaming bloody murder," Izzy threatened, not daunted in the least by the man's authoritative manner.

"Funny you should put it quite that way," Steve let out a humorless chuckle, and shoved against the door in a lightning-fast motion that had Izzy on her backside and him in her foyer before she knew what was happening.

"You get out of my house this instant," she screeched in fury and reached for her phone, which had skittered away from her on impact.

"That's not going to happen," Steve replied calmly, after he executed a series of ninja-like moves that had the author lying on her stomach, arms between her shoulder blades, immobile. "It would have been so much easier on you if you had just played nice and let me in," he sighed with mock regret. "I suppose I should've expected no less from someone who had the poor judgment to associate with the likes of Bengal."

"I'm not associated with Spencer Bengal," Izzy growled between her teeth. "And if you're from the government, you'd better believe I'm going to be reporting this to whomever needs to know about it. I hope you're familiar with the unemployment line."

"Oh, little kitten… it's adorable that you're trying to threaten me, it really is, but I'm afraid I don't have time to waste on arguing with you, so we're just going to have to handle this a different way."

Steve pulled a vial out of his pocket, unscrewed the cap, holding it away from his face, and saturated a cloth with it. He placed the sweet-smelling cloth over Izzy's nose and mouth, and despite thrashing and struggling to avoid it, she succumbed and lay still within minutes. Steve slipped the saturated cloth into a plastic bag, which he placed back in his pocket, along with the empty vial, for disposal later, and hoisted the limp author to her feet as though she weighed nothing. He used her hand to turn the doorknob to let them out of the house, then used it to close it behind them. Swinging her up into his arms, he laid her head on his shoulder, and began laughing loudly. As he walked with her to his car, he held up what looked like his half of a conversation.

"And then I say to the guy, if the blonde in the bar had a dog, did that mean she was available?" and he dissolved into another gale of fake laughter. He pressed a button on a fob and the passenger door of the expensive Italian sports car popped open. Pretending to kiss Izzy deeply, he lowered her into the car and shut the door behind her, saying, "Don't worry, sweetheart, there's lots more where that came from."

The car's windows were heavily tinted, so any neighbors who happened to be peering out from between their blinds at the spectacle, wouldn't see that Izzy Gilmore was lying unconscious in the passenger seat.

CHAPTER FIFTEEN

"Jeanette Hammond is involved with the mob?" Missy whispered, wide-eyed, as she sat across the table from Chas at a Japanese fusion restaurant in downtown Champaign.

"I don't know if she is or not, but it certainly seems like the men she dates may be," Chas replied quietly.

They were seated in a remote corner of the restaurant, at the detective's request, where they could talk without being overheard.

"What makes you think that Stanton and Tommy are involved in the mob?"

"For one thing, on paper, Stanton is a very middle of the road accountant, which makes it very strange that he lives in an exclusive neighborhood, travels the globe, and owns a lake house, a boat, and plenty of other expensive luxury items. He also came from Chicago, and has some clients who seem shady to say the least," Chas explained.

"Shady? Shady how?" Missy asked, popping a piece of sushi in her mouth.

"Shady like a dry cleaner who cleared fourteen million in profits last year alone."

"Sounds like they're laundering something more than dirty shirts," Missy quipped, raising an eyebrow.

"Exactly," Chas nodded, splitting open an edamame pod and sucking out the contents.

"What about Tommy?"

"He's Italian, he's dating a woman who may be associated with someone in the mob, and he's been in jail. Two plus two generally makes four," the detective shrugged.

Missy dropped her chopsticks in astonishment. "Chas Beckett, that's profiling," she accused, her mouth hanging open.

"I'm not saying he's a criminal, or that he's involved in anything even remotely illegal, it's just that he has interesting connections that should probably be investigated."

She sighed deeply and picked up her chopsticks again. "Yeah, I know. I've been suspicious of him too. How did you find out about all of this?" she asked, feeling guilty.

"Kel filled me in when we figured out that you might be in grave danger, and I did some investigating of my own."

"I'm really sorry that I didn't tell you what we were up to. I just thought we'd find Jeanette, get Scott back home to his mother, and everyone would be happy. I had no idea what we were getting ourselves into," Missy admitted, reaching for her husband's hand.

"Sweetie, you're smart, and brave, and you always want to go the extra mile for the people you love, and I love that about you, but you're going to have to learn to trust me with this stuff. I don't know what I'd do if anything happened to you," Chas said softly, bringing her hand to his lips, and letting them linger there for a moment.

"I'm sorry," Missy whispered, moving into his embrace.

"I know," her husband held her and kissed the top of her head.

She sat back after a moment, gazing into his eyes. "What do we do now?"

"Now, we finish our dinner, then we're going to go enjoy the hot tub at the hotel, and in the morning, we'll pay Tommy and Stanton another visit."

***

Tommy Mancino wiped his hands on a shop towel, and dropped it onto the counter, shaking his head when he saw Missy and Chas approaching.

"Geez lady, are you going to stalk me forever now?" he said with a smile.

"I'm sorry to bother you again, Mr. Mancino, but I wanted to introduce you to my husband, Chas. Do you have a minute to talk?"

Tommy eyed Chas thoughtfully. "You're a cop. Vice or homicide?" he asked, not smiling, but not hostile either.

"Homicide."

"You ain't local," the mechanic observed.

"Nope," Chas agreed easily.

"Whaddya want with me?"

"I want to talk about Jeanette Hammond. Tell me what happened the last time you saw her."

Tommy looked from Chas to Missy and back again, then over at Sal, who was watching them curiously from the other side of the auto bay.

"Let's go into the office for a minute," Mancino suggested.

Chas nodded and he and Missy followed the mechanic inside.

"First of all, I don't know where she is or what happened to her. For all I know, she could be hanging out in one of Vincenzo's houses overseas," he shrugged.

"You know Vincenzo?"

"I know OF him. We don't exactly travel in the same circles," Tommy replied dryly.

"When's the last time you saw Jeanette?"

"She and her friend dropped her car off her so that I could work on it. She gave me the keys, I told her I'd call her when it was ready, and that was it."

"Her friend? What friend?"

"The redhead, the realtor chick."

"Rhonda," Missy said softly.

"Yeah, Ronnie. She and Jeanie work together, they're pretty tight."

"What do you know about Rhonda?" Chas asked.

"Not much. Nice chick. I went out with her once, there was just nothing there, ya know what I mean? She's got a good job, she's pretty and all, but she just wasn't my type."

"Sure, it happens," the detective nodded. "Did Jeanette give you any indication that she might be going out of town, or that she might have to leave her car here for a period of time?"

"Nope, she just said that she'd pick it up when it was done. The two of them drove off in Ronnie's car and I haven't seen either of them since."

"Does the name Ricky Raguso mean anything to you?"

Tommy's eyes narrowed.

"Everybody's heard of the Raccoon, why?"

"Does he work for Vincenzo?"

Mancino rolled his eyes and smirked.

"Raguso works for anybody who'll pay him. You think he's got Jeanie?" he asked, suddenly sobering. "Cuz if the Raccoon got her, she ain't gonna last long. When he gets 'em, they stay got."

"That's what I'm trying to find out," Chas said grimly.

***

"See what I mean?" Missy said after they left Sal's Garage. "Tommy may be a bit rough around the edges, but he doesn't strike me as being the bad guy."

"I have to agree," Chas nodded. "He didn't hesitate when he was answering questions, none of his body language indicated that he might be lying, and he didn't get hostile, even though he knew immediately that I was a detective. I think he's on the up and up."

"Which leaves us with Stanton Vincenzo," Missy sighed.

"Exactly."

"Are you going to talk to him?"

"I don't see that I have any choice, but you're not going to come along when I do. I don't want you anywhere around Vincenzo, and I definitely don't want him to know that you're a detective's wife. I'll drop you off at the hotel, then I'll stop by to see him."

"What can I do in the meantime?"

"See if you can get in touch with Kel and get some information about Rhonda the realtor. I may want to talk with her as well, to get a better idea of Jeanette's habits, hangouts, and anything else that might help us reconstruct where she was and what she was doing when she disappeared."

"So, you think that Kel and I were right not to go to the police?" Missy asked.

"I think that you and Kel did a very dangerous thing," Chas gave her a reproving look. "But, unfortunately, now that it looks like we might be dealing with organized crime, it probably is safer for Jeanette if we don't involve the local police."

They arrived at the hotel, and Chas escorted Missy to the room, checking it out thoroughly before allowing her to enter.

"Lock the doors, don't let anyone know that you're in here, and see what you can find out from Kel," the detective instructed, kissing his wife at the door.

"Just come back safe," she whispered, hugging him tightly before he left.

"Always," he winked.

***

"I'm here to see Stanton Vincenzo," Chas flashed his badge briefly at the receptionist, whose eyes went wide.

"Is he expecting you?" she asked, doing her job despite being intimidated by the handsome detective in front of her.

"No, but I believe he'll want to have this conversation," Chas replied coolly.

Vincenzo appeared from the inner sanctum as though by magic.

"Good afternoon, Officer. What can I help you with?" Stanton asked with a smile. The man was clearly accustomed to showing a polite poker face at a moment's notice.

"It's 'Detective,' and I'd like to speak with you about Jeanette Hammond," Chas stared him down, well aware of the doe-eyed receptionist watching his every move.

"Let's go to my office," Vincenzo led the way, his cheerful demeanor never wavering for a second, at least until they were seated on opposite sides of his desk.

The accountant studied Chas closely, fingers tented under his chin.

"You come in here, asking questions in front of the help, and you ain't even local. Who are you, and what are you doing in my town, asking questions?" Stanton's eyes narrowed.

"I'm someone who is looking out for the best interests of Jeanette Hammond, not that that's any of your business, and I'm thinking you just might know where she is and why she disappeared without bothering to tell anyone," the detective was entirely undaunted by the mobster's hostility.

"I don't know nothing," Vincenzo met the detective's gaze evenly. "I hooked up with her for a while. She was neurotic, didn't know how to have a relationship, and was married to her work. End of story. I wasn't thrilled with her after that, I'll tell ya, but I didn't make her disappear," Stanton shrugged.

"Then who did? Raguso?" Chas persisted, glaring at the accountant.

"Raguso?" Vincenzo laughed. "Raguso is small-time. He don't do nothing on his own. If Raguso's got her, somebody else is paying for it. If you think the Raccoon is involved, you better start looking at her life and finding out who wants her dead, cuz that's what he does. That's ALL he does."

"Does Tommy Mancino want her dead?"

"He'd be on the list, I would think. She may have cut him loose, cuz he wasn't good enough for the likes of her, who knows. The broad couldn't commit. She could have all kinds of frustrated exes who are out to get her, all I know is I ain't one of 'em. I got options, if you know what I mean," he smirked.

"I'm sure you do," Chas rolled his eyes.

***

Missy had called the real estate office where Jeanette Hammond worked and had made an appointment to meet with Jeanette's teammate and friend, Rhonda the next morning. She and Chas sat in the driveway of the vacant mini-mansion, and eventually saw her pull up in the same luxury sedan that she'd been driving when she'd arrived at Jeanette's house, interrupting Missy and Kel's search.

"Hi!" the high-maintenance redhead sang out. "You must be Mindy and Robert. I'm Rhonda, it's so nice to meet you."

Chas shot Missy a look which clearly indicated that she should have told him that she'd used assumed names, and they followed the trail of perfume into the home.

"Rhonda, I just want to be really up front with you about why we're here. Jeanette is a friend of mine from high school, and I haven't heard from her in a couple of weeks… I'm really worried about her, and I know that she's close with you, she talks about you all the time, so I was hoping that you might know where she is," Missy confided, placing a hand on Rhonda's arm.

"Oh honey, that's sweet. Why didn't you just come by my office?" the realtor replied, touching a hand to her hair.

"Well, I thought that maybe… if it was something embarrassing, like that she'd run off with a guy or something, that it'd be easier, and kinder, to talk about it where no one could overhear," Missy lied beautifully.

"Well, aren't you considerate," Rhonda smiled. "Honestly, I don't know what to make of this whole thing," she shook her head. "She's gone away to be by herself every once in a while, but never for this length of time. There were appointments that she had scheduled with clients, and the rest of us on the team had to cover for her, which is fine, but it's just not like her to neglect her work like that."

163

"Do you know where she might be, or who she might be with?" Chas asked.

"I wish I knew. The only person that I'm worried about is a guy named Tommy Mancino. She dated him occasionally, and..." she leaned in close, despite the fact that they were alone. "He's an ex-convict," she whispered and pressed her lips together in disapproval.

"Do you know Tommy?" Missy asked.

"Well, you know..." Rhonda waved a hand airily. "Everyone kinda knows everyone else in this town. He has *quite* the reputation with the ladies," she raised her eyebrows and nodded knowingly.

"But you don't think he'd hurt Jeanie, do you?"

"I honestly don't know. I hope not, but I just don't know."

"Have you ever heard of Ricky Raguso?"

"Nope, but the name sounds delicious," Rhonda chuckled.

"Yeah, it kinda does," Missy tried not to cringe. "Do you know some of the places where Jeanie used to hang out? Could there be someone who might have seen her, or might know where she went?"

"I doubt it," Rhonda shook her head. "Jeanette was a very private person, as you know. She never went out alone, and whenever she did go out, I was with her. I've asked at all the places we used to go to together, and no one has seen or heard from her."

"Has anyone called the police?"

"Well, I did the other day, because I went over to check on her house, and there was a strange car parked in the driveway," Rhonda confided.

"Did the police get any leads?" Chas asked.

"Not that I know of. They just said that the car was a rental, but they didn't tell me anything else."

Missy tried again. "Did you go inside at all?"

"Yep, Jeanie gave me a key, so that if she ever needed anything done while she was traveling or whatever, I'd be able to take care of it for her. I didn't see anything broken or missing. Nothing looked out of place."

"I wonder where her son is." Missy murmured.

"My guess would be that he's with her. Maybe she just took him on a nice long summer vacation."

"Does she tend to be impulsive like that?" Chas broke in again.

"Occasionally. Jeanie is a hard egg to crack, you never know what's going on in that head of hers."

"That's Jeanie all right," Missy nodded, remembering to keep up the ruse. "Well, thank you, Rhonda, I hope it wasn't too much of an intrusion for you to meet us out here."

"Not at all," the realtor smiled. "Any friend of Jeanie's is a friend of mine."

***

"Well, that seemed like a colossal waste of time," Missy lamented when they got back into Chas's rental car and watched Rhonda drive away with a manicured wave.

"Maybe," Chas replied, distracted.

"Rhonda and Stanton think that Tommy is the bad guy, Tommy thinks Stanton is the bad guy, and Tommy and Stanton both think that Ricky Raguso is scum. What are we going to do?" Missy sighed.

"The only thing that I can think of is to try to find Ricky Raguso."

CHAPTER SIXTEEN

Joyce Rutledge unlocked the door to the bookstore and candle shop, humming to herself. Spencer had joined her for ribs, beans, potato salad, cornbread, and her sour cream chocolate cake last night. After dinner she'd popped a silly comedy DVD in, and they'd both enjoyed some much-needed laughter. He'd been a perfect gentleman, and hadn't even attempted to hold her hand before he left, which was unfortunate, but Joyce was hopeful that the shy Marine might just open up eventually.

She flipped on all the lights, using the main breaker in the office, and made coffee, enjoying the gurgling sounds which promised that the rich, dark brew was soon on its way. While she was waiting for her coffee, the chimes over the door sounded, which was odd at this early hour. They weren't supposed to open for another hour and a half, Joyce just preferred to arrive early to make certain that everything was ready to go when customers started showing up.

She made her way to the front, calling out, "Hello?" with no response.

"Hmm... that's weird," she muttered to herself, her eyes darting here and there, looking for an early bird in the aisles of books and candles.

Walking over to the front door, she saw a small brown box. Apparently a delivery had been made and the service hadn't waited around for a signature. She picked up the box and set it on the counter, pulling open a drawer and finding a box cutter to open the package. It was addressed to Echo, but since Echo had asked her to open and process all deliveries while she was gone, she slit open the seams, resheathed and set the box cutter back in the drawer. She folded the flaps back and screamed, then ran for the bathroom and deposited her breakfast in the nearest stall.

After she pulled herself together, rinsing out her mouth, washing her face, and pouring a strong cup of coffee with shaking hands, Joyce dialed 911. Officer Emil Bergen arrived ten minutes later, and found the shaken manager sitting on a bench in the fiction section, trembling. The sign on the door to both shops still said "Closed," and probably would for the remainder of the day at least.

She told the officer what had happened, and he took notes, then put the entire box into a cooler, taking it into evidence.

"Do you have any idea who might have sent this?" Officer Bergen asked.

"No sir," Joyce shook her head, pulse still racing, bile stinging the back of her throat, even after coffee.

"Does your boss have any enemies that you know of?"

"I don't know how she could. She's just about the nicest person you could ever meet."

"Where is she now?"

"I'm not sure. She went on vacation with her fiancé, I think."

"How long will she be gone?"

"I don't know."

"Do you have contact info for her?" the officer persisted.

"Yes, sir," Joyce replied, giving it to him.

"Thank you Miss Rutledge," he said, handing her his business card. "If you think of anything else, let me know."

"I sure will," she nodded. "Officer?"

"Yes ma'am?"

"Do you think... I mean, am I... should I... ?" she couldn't quite think of a way to phrase her question, she was so rattled, but the veteran cop knew what she was asking.

"I don't think you have anything to worry about, since the package wasn't addressed to you, but take some extra precautions just in case. Try not to arrive or leave in the dark. Lock the doors when you're not open for business, and just keep your eyes peeled for anything that seems suspicious."

"Okay, thank you," Joyce shook Bergen's hand. "I'm going to go home for the rest of today, but I'll be open tomorrow."

"Good luck to you. We'll be in touch if we need anything else."

She waited until the police cruiser had pulled away from the curb before sending Spencer a text.

I have a very strange story to tell you tonight, and I'm a little scared, can you come over?

***

County medical examiner and Calgon's strangest and most prominent mortician, Timothy Eckels, snapped on his blue nitrile gloves and accepted the package from Officer Bergen. His spunky assistant Fiona had a glimmer in her eye, wondering what the plain brown box held that was so important that they'd called Tim out of a high-profile funeral. While her boss held the camera that he used for forensic photography, she pushed the flaps of the box back with her gloved hands, her mouth making an O of surprise when she saw the contents. Wrapped in plastic wrap, lying on a bed of Styrofoam peanuts was a woman's finger, complete with a perfectly manicured acrylic nail.

Tim's face was impassive as he studied the finger, taking it out of the box to get several shots of it with the camera, from many different angles. Officer Bergen left once the medical examiner began his process, and Fiona was practically dancing with excitement.

"Oooh! Can I unwrap it, please? I know you have to unwrap it to examine it, can I do it?" she practically begged. Fiona's boss was the best in his field and she soaked up every bit of information that she could from him, often intentionally ruffling his feathers in the process.

"No. The digit must be handled properly so that any evidence that may exist isn't disturbed," he replied mildly, still snapping photos.

"I handle digits at the mortuary all the time, c'mon," she wheedled.

"The digits at the mortuary aren't part of a crime investigation," was the implacable response from her bespectacled, taciturn superior.

"I wonder who did it... I wonder how they did it," she mused, peering at the finger.

Tim looked offended and blinked at her from behind his coke-bottle lenses.

"This is why I can't trust you with evidentiary material yet," he shook his head, gesturing at the finger lying on the cold metal exam table. "Clearly it was sheared off cleanly, rather than being chopped or sawn," he pointed out. "As to the question of who did it, we'll take scrapings from beneath the nail to see if there's DNA present. You should know these things."

"I do know these things," she muttered as Tim unwrapped the finger carefully. "I just never get to do them."

"And you never will if you continue to distract me," he replied mildly, squinting down at the finger, turning it back and forth. "Well, there is a bit of good news for the owner of the finger," he mused.

"What's that?" Fiona drew in closer, her eyes fastened on the finger.

"She's still alive. Or, at least, she *was* when it was removed from her hand."

"Creepy," Fiona breathed. "Can you tell if she was awake? Did it hurt? How come it's not all bloody?" she peppered her reticent boss with questions.

"Those things are irrelevant. What matters here is that there is a victim out there somewhere, missing a finger, and she may still be alive."

***

Chas and Missy were sitting in the airport in Champaign, waiting for their flight, when the detective received a text from dispatch in Calgon. He sighed and shook his head, and Missy asked what was wrong.

"A box was delivered to Echo's store. It contained a woman's severed finger, and I'm betting it belongs to Jeanette Hammond. Things appear to be escalating."

"Oh Chas, no! Does that mean that she's… ?"

"The M.E. says that the finger was severed while the victim was still alive, that's a good sign. Someone is trying to send a message of some sort. They don't necessarily want to kill Jeanette."

"What do they want, then?" Missy's eyes went wide.

"That's what we have to find out… and quickly."

CHAPTER SEVENTEEN

Missy was shocked to see Echo walk in to Cupcakes in Paradise the day after she and Chas returned home to Calgon.

"Sugar, what are you doing here?" she exclaimed. "I thought you and the boys were hiding out somewhere," her brow furrowed in concern.

"We were," she sighed. "But apparently, whoever is tormenting us is better at seeking than we are at hiding."

"They found you? How do you know? Did something happen?" Missy worried, sitting down at their favorite table.

"This was inside our hotel room when we came back in from a hike," she said dully, tossing a creamy white envelope, which had been mailed from Chicago, onto the table.

Missy moved quickly to the kitchen, pulled on a pair of plastic gloves, and handled the envelope gingerly, extracting the piece of paper within it.

Leave it alone and forget about her.

She read the chilling message and looked up at a pale, tired Echo.

"This is getting ridiculous, honey," she said quietly. "I really think that it's time to go to the police with this."

Echo shook her head. "I don't want to do anything that might put Jeanette in danger."

"But it sounds to me like you and Kel and Scott may be the ones in danger, and I hate to say it, but for all we know, Jeanette may not even be alive right now."

Missy went to put the paper back in the envelope and stopped suddenly, staring at something inside the envelope. She shook it slightly, and her eyes grew wide.

"What?" Echo asked, head in hand, noting her friend's reaction.

"There's something..." Missy trailed off, shaking the envelope again.

"What?" Echo stood up, peering over Missy's shoulder.

"There, see it?"

Echo looked at her friend, and back into the envelope again. "A hair!" she exclaimed. "Do you have tweezers?"

"I think there's a pair in the top drawer of my desk, run and get them," Missy murmured, tapping the edge of the envelope to make the hair more accessible.

Echo came back with the tweezers and Missy gently extracted the hair from the envelope.

"Oh," Echo sighed, disappointed. "It looks like one of mine."

Missy shook her head. "Nope, no way. Yours is curly, this one is wavy, and yours is a beautiful shade of copper, this one is a totally different shade of red. We should have Chas see if he can discreetly check it out in the lab. Maybe Ricky the Raccoon has an accomplice."

"I just don't understand why the mob would be interested in Jeanette Hammond," Echo frowned.

"I don't either, but maybe this clue will make things clearer somehow."

"It's worth a shot," she shrugged, looking exhausted.

"You poor thing, you've been through the wringer lately. Wanna go lay down by the pool today? I can come over and join you after I close up here this afternoon," Missy offered, putting the hair back into the envelope and texting Chas.

"No, I need to get to the shop. Joyce was pretty freaked out, so I told her that she could have today off."

"Is Spencer going to help you out?"

Echo nodded. "I saw him working on the lawn mower on my way in, so I stopped and asked him. Honestly, Missy, I don't know what I'm going to do when you and Chas move to New York, and Spencer goes wherever he's going... we're a family, and it seems like everything is just falling apart," her voice broke, and a single tear trickled down her cheek.

Missy brushed the tear away and hugged her best friend.

"I know, I'm going to miss Spencer too—that boy is like a son to me, but don't you worry, I'm going to be back and forth between New York and Calgon so often that you're going to get tired of having me around," she promised.

"I can't do this whole birth and motherhood thing without you," Echo sniffled against her shoulder.

"And you won't have to, darlin, I'm gonna be right here."

***

Chas took the envelope with the hair to the lab, along with a sample of Echo's hair for comparison purposes.

"Don't you think that it's strange that Jeanette is missing—and clearly someone has her—and is threatening Kel and her son, but there haven't been any demands made?" Missy asked Chas. "I mean, no one has asked for money or anything, isn't that weird? Aren't kidnappings usually motivated by the desire for something else?"

The detective nodded. "Typically, yes. Usually the kidnapper wants something, whether it's money or power, or political influence, but that doesn't seem to be the case here."

"What other things can motivate a kidnapper?" Missy wondered, sipping her wine as she snuggled into the crook of her husband's arm on the couch.

"Depends on the kidnapper. Revenge, jealousy, narcissism, control… there's a wide range of human emotion that could prompt an unstable person to take action," Chas commented, nuzzling his wife's hair.

"Well, yeah, but who on earth would be vengeful toward or envious of a middle-aged, middle-class mom who sells houses?"

A thought occurred to Missy as the words left her mouth, and she turned to Chas, who had clearly had the same thought. Realization had dawned on both of them at the same time, and they shared a long look.

"I'm guessing that you're flying back to Champaign tomorrow," the detective commented, his face grave.

"You can't go with me?"

"Unfortunately, no. But I'll want you to stay in contact with me every step of the way," he cupped her cheek in his palm and kissed her gently.

"I will."

***

Missy checked back into the downtown hotel where she'd stayed before, and wasted no time in heading over to Sal's Garage.

"Are we besties now?" Tommy Mancino joked when he saw Missy.

"We're getting there," she grinned, glad that she no longer had to be afraid of the mechanic. If her hunch was correct, not only did she not have to worry about being around Tommy, but she might be able to use him to trap the real kidnapper… if he was willing. "Can we talk privately?"

"Is that a proposition?" he teased.

"Of sorts," Missy shot back, following him into the office.

There was a small television on the back counter in the office, which was currently tuned to a local news channel, and the report that was on the screen caught Missy's attention.

"Turn it up," she ordered, suddenly serious.

In other news... the body of a local woman, who died under suspicious circumstances, was found today near a vacant house in the rural community of Saint Joe. Identification has been made, but will not be released, pending notification of the victim's family. Police are currently investigating...

Missy swallowed hard, somehow knowing in her gut that the woman who'd been killed was Jeanette Hammond.

"You all right, Mindy?" Tommy asked, noticing how Missy had paled after watching the newscast.

Unable to speak, she just shook her head.

***

William "Billy Boy" MacGregor had been in the real estate business for a long time, and he'd encountered his share of difficult clients, but the ones that he'd been chauffeuring around for the past couple of weeks, really took the cake. They were very specific about what they were looking for, and found something wrong with every property that he'd shown them in and around Champaign.

"Now, this one is a little bit further out, so you'd have to commute, but I think it has everything that you're looking for. It's on a full acre, and your nearest neighbor is about a half mile away. It has big trees for shade, a pond, and plenty of space for the kids to play. There are five bedrooms, so that your yorkies can have their own room, and the master suite is on the first floor. The décor is a bit dated, but you've said you'd want to repaint and update any house that you'd move into anyhow, so this might just be the one," Billy Boy said, hoping that the house worked out.

He'd shown them every listing he could think of, and nothing had met with their approval. At this point, he wanted them to find a place simply so he could stop driving them all over central Illinois, listening to them complain. The couple had five yorkies, four of which were back home in Olympia, Washington. The fifth, Francis, they had brought house-hunting with them. They'd rejected two homes so far because Francis wasn't "comfortable enough in the yard to even lift his leg." Billy Boy loved dogs in general, but would have been more than happy to let Francis stay napping in the car while his owners made a human-based decision. The dog was obnoxious, running from room to room in every house that they toured, most of the time barking to announce his presence, but the owners insisted that if Francis wasn't comfortable, they wouldn't buy, so he stocked up on gluten-free, organic dog treats and made the best of it.

"Here we are," he said, handing the husband, a rotund man with thinning hair, a listing sheet, while the wife peered at the house from the back seat of his SUV, absently petting Francis. "Shall we?"

"Francis wants to get out of the car, I guess that's a good sign," the wife observed.

Billy Boy gritted his teeth and smiled. "Well, sounds like we're halfway there. Let's go have a look," he encouraged, wondering this particular couple had chosen him from online realtors.

He opened up the house, leaving the front door slightly ajar, and took the couple through, gratified to see some nodding, and even a couple of smiles. Francis yapped happily, and dashed throughout the large house, making himself at home, walking across furniture, and sniffing every corner. The couple was upstairs, discussing potential furniture arrangements for a children's playroom, always a good buying sign, when they noticed that they hadn't seen Francis for quite some time. They called his name several times, making little kissy noises that usually made him come running, and became alarmed when he didn't appear. They dashed down the stairs and called his name again, relieved to hear him yapping, though it sounded like he was quite a distance away. Rushing out the front door, the wife put a hand over her eyes to block the sun, and called for Francis again. This time it was evident that the yapped response came from behind the house, and the trio trotted around the side, seeing Francis digging up the ground in front of a clump of bushes like his little life depended on it.

"Francis! No! You're going to break a nail, stop that," the wife scolded, crossing the great expanse of yard between the back of the house and the clump of bushes which lined the edge of the large property.

"Francis, down boy," the husband gasped, trying his best to keep up with his wife's longer stride, the back of his shirt darkened with sweat.

She was too fast for him, however, and reached the little dog before her husband and the realtor, who had adopted a slower pace to keep the larger man company on the walk. When she neared the bushes, her hands went to her throat in horror and she screamed long and loud, plucking her yapping, dirty little dog up in a panic and running pell mell back toward the house, not stopping when she reached the two men, but sprinting past them toward the front of the house.

Billy Boy and the husband stopped and stared after her, then looked at each other, nonplussed.

"Wonder what that's all about," the realtor commented.

"Why don't you go check it out, and I'll go talk to her," the husband puffed, turning and heading back toward the car.

"Sure, I'd love to. It's in my job description. That's why they pay me the big bucks," Billy Boy muttered under his breath once the large, sweaty client was out of earshot.

He trudged over to where the dog had been digging, disgusted that yet again the furry little beast had ruined the chance to sell a perfectly good house, and when he saw what the dog had discovered, he paled and stopped in his tracks. In the midst of the freshly dug earth was a pale woman's foot, partially covered in a tattered silk stocking. Knowing that this was a story he'd tell to new agents for the rest of his career, he numbly reached into his pocket for his phone and called the police.

***

"Tommy, you're going to help me catch a murderer, not a kidnapper," Missy whispered, looking away from the TV after the newscast ended.

CHAPTER EIGHTEEN

Rhonda Cooper smiled coyly and tried hard not to bat her eyes at the handsome hunk of a man sitting across from her at the bar. She'd worn her sexiest dress, splurged on a new pair of black patent leather heels, which were currently destroying her feet, and had swept her red hair up into an intricate up-do that exposed the creamy curve of her neck. Yep, Rhonda the realtor was working it with Tommy Mancino, who had finally invited her out for a date, just as she'd been expecting him to.

"You look beautiful," he raised his glass to her and took a sip of a very dirty martini. Her eyes had seemed to glow when he ordered it.

She blushed, knowing that it was true. "Well, aren't you sweet! You're not so bad yourself... thanks for giving me a call."

"My pleasure," he nodded, flirting.

"So, what took you so long, handsome?"

"Well, I was kinda seeing your friend, ya know, and I thought that I might see her again, but when she didn't answer my texts for like three weeks, I figured that she was sending a pretty clear message," he shrugged.

"I'd say so," Rhonda nodded, her lips pursed. "I mean, that's just rude. If I'm not interested in a man, I just let him know. I don't lead him on and then stop responding."

"You don't think she'll be mad, do you?" Tommy asked, popping an olive that he scooped out of the martini into his mouth.

"I can almost guarantee she won't," Rhonda smiled a strange smile.

"I almost didn't ask you out, ya know."

"Because you thought that someone who had ignored you might be mad? That's just silly," she snorted.

"No, because I heard somebody else had dibs on you."

"What? I'm not seeing anyone else," she frowned. "Who would've said such a thing?"

"Ricky Raguso," Tommy went after another olive.

An expression that looked like a mix of fury and terror flickered momentarily across Rhonda's features, so briefly that if he hadn't been looking for it, he probably never would have seen it.

"Ricky... what? I've never heard of that person," she stammered, taking a gulp of her manhattan.

Tommy set his drink down and raised his eyebrows. "Well, he's sure as heck heard of you. Said he did some work for you, and that you might have a thing going on. Said you hit on him pretty hard," he shrugged.

"Well, that's preposterous..." Rhonda sputtered, clearly rattled. "I work with a lot of different contractors, and I don't hit on any of them, so if he said that, clearly he's an egotistical, delusional maniac," she exclaimed.

"That's a pretty harsh thing to say about someone you don't even remember," he observed, reaching into a bowl of peanuts, shelling one, and tossing the salty halves in his mouth.

"Well... men shouldn't be spreading rumors like that about women that they work for. It's just offensive."

"What did he do for you?"

"I have no idea. I don't remember. He could've been a pest control inspector for all I know," she glanced away, taking another swig of her drink.

"Well, I'm sure you know, I have a bit of a 'checkered' past," Tommy began, watching her carefully. "And I gotta tell ya, the things I heard about Ricky while I was in the joint are pretty scary for a delicate lady like you."

"What do you mean? Should I be concerned for my safety?" she asked, blinking rapidly, and gesturing to the bartender for a refill.

"What I mean is that when Ricky does work for people, somebody certainly better be worried about their safety," Tommy smirked.

"I don't know what you're talking about," Rhonda covered her discomfort by fishing the cherry out of her new drink and eating it.

Tommy moved closer. He was able to tell by her eye movements and expression that the liquor was kicking in, and he was going to make the most of it.

"Look doll, I'm flattered, okay?" he whispered in her ear, letting his lips graze the side of her neck. He heard the sharp intake of her breath and knew that he was on the right track.

"I think you and me will make a good team. Whatever you had to do to make that happen, can't be a bad thing, right?" he continued, touching her lower lip with a fingertip, then kissing her briefly.

"Really?" she breathed, unable to think straight with the man of her dreams behaving this way.

"Yeah baby. The way I see it, getting Jeanie out of the way opened my eyes to… greater possibilities," he kissed the side of her neck, feeling her pulse race beneath his lips. "Mmm…" he groaned. "You smell good."

"It's Jeanie's perfume," Rhonda confessed, her head spinning with alcohol and lust.

"It smells better on you," Tommy purred, running his fingertips along her jawline, making her forget that they were in a very public place. "Did you take it after you offed her?"

"I didn't do it," Rhonda gasped, grabbing a handful of his thick black hair.

"Ricky did it?" he nibbled her earlobe, making her groan.

"Mmhmm…" she murmured, sinking her fingernails into Tommy's biceps.

"How much did you pay him, sweetheart? I'll give you back every dime, I swear," he took her hand, kissing her palm and moving his lips up to the tender skin in the crook of her elbow.

"Don't worry, it wasn't much," she whispered. "He only asked for twenty grand, and I took it out of the safe in Jeanie's office. I couldn't stand not being with you…"

Tommy pulled back for a moment, brushing a strand of hair from Rhonda's eyes and staring into them intently.

"You only had to give Ricky twenty grand to off Jeanie, and you used her own money to do it?" he grinned with admiration.

"Yes," she nodded, spellbound. "I did it for you, Tommy, for us. I knew I couldn't have you as long as she was in the way. I've wanted you for so long," she confessed, licking her upper teeth in a way that she thought was seductive.

"Wow," Tommy Mancino nodded. "Rhonda, baby?"

"Yes," she said breathlessly.

He leaned over until his lips brushed her ear and his breath stirred her hair. "You're under arrest."

Police rushed in from every side, while Tommy made sure that Rhonda Cooper didn't go anywhere.

"You tricked me," she said as he lifted his shirt to untape the wire that he'd been wearing, while she was being handcuffed. "You're no good, Tommy Mancino. I should've known better. Ricky warned me about you, said you were nothing but trouble, said he'd off you, too. For free if I wanted. I should've let him. I should've paid him to go after you," she screamed hysterically.

Tommy shook his head and met Missy's eyes across the bar. She nodded her thanks and slipped out a side door, ready to go home to her husband, and to help Echo and Kel console a grieving teenager who'd lost his mother.

CHAPTER NINETEEN

"I now pronounce you man and wife, you may kiss your bride," Judge Harlan Campbell proclaimed, beaming at Echo and Kel.

Scott stood by his father's side, holding up amazingly well after having buried his mother a month earlier. Missy, Chas, Spencer, and Joyce attended the courthouse nuptials as well, the women wiping tears, the men grinning at the couple's happiness. Maggie the innkeeper, in charge of events as usual, was at the inn overseeing the efforts of the caterer. While Echo and Kel had nixed plans for a full-blown reception, Missy had managed to talk them into at least letting her host a celebratory dinner at the inn for close friends and family, and the Wedgwood parlor had been transformed into a fairyland of twinkling lights, candles, beautiful china and crystal, featuring an orchestral trio that would play love songs during the event.

The dinner had just begun when Spencer felt a chill running down his spine and turned to see one of the waiters from the catering company studying him closely. When he recognized the man, his face remained neutral, despite his profound internal reaction.

"Excuse me for a moment," he said graciously, standing and buttoning the jacket on his tuxedo.

Kel had insisted that, though they might be having "just a courthouse wedding," the men would wear tuxedos, and the women would wear formal dresses. There were some compromises that he just wouldn't make, and not wearing a tuxedo to his wedding was one of them.

"Everything okay?" Missy asked, instantly alert.

"Yes, everything is fine," he smiled, his glance lingering on Joyce for a moment. "I'm just going to go check on Maggie and make sure she has everything under control.

"Okay, darlin, and could you make sure that we ordered enough champagne?"

"Of course," the Marine smiled and headed for the kitchen, the waiter that he had spotted close at his heels.

"What are you doing here?" Spencer hissed once he'd reached the deserted butler's pantry.

His long-time colleague, Janssen, a scarred veteran who also worked for Beckett Holdings' security division moved closer, so that what he had to say wouldn't be overheard.

"Steve Arnold is in town," he said in a low, urgent voice. "I'm here because I knew we'd both be safer in the same place and I had to let you know."

"What does he want?" Spencer's jaw was set in a chiseled line.

"What does he always want, man? He probably was sent to bring you in for an assignment."

"How do you know that he's not here looking for you?"

"My sources say it's you, but you know how it goes, if he can't get you, he'll probably settle for me," Janssen shrugged with a grimace.

"How are we going to approach this?" Spencer's eyes darted back and forth as he considered various possibilities.

"I say we beat him at his own game," the scarred Marine suggested.

"What do you mean?" Spencer eyed him guardedly.

"He's always trying to convince us to go back to black ops. Tells us that the best way we can serve our country is by staying anonymous and going on suicide missions. What if we recruit him to do what we do? What if we make him a team member for Beckett Holdings? With the connections that he's got, it'd make our lives a lot easier, and we wouldn't have to constantly be looking over our shoulders. Simple."

Spencer stared at Janssen for a long moment. "Have you lost your mind completely? Steve Arnold doesn't care whether we live or die as long as he has warm bodies for his off-the-book suicide missions, and you want to try to convince him to serve the greater good by coming to work with us? Did you get too close to a concussion grenade recently?"

Janssen quirked an eyebrow.

"I'm serious here. If you can't beat 'em, join 'em. Or, in this case, have 'em join us instead. Think about it, Bengal, if black ops doesn't have Steve birddogging us for them, they'll give up and leave us alone. They're certainly not going to spend the funds that it would require to train someone who would be able to find us and deliver us to HQ for an assignment."

"We can't make that assumption. If taking Steve Arnold out of commission would've accomplished that, someone would've done it a long time ago."

"Well, clearly, time is running short, and we're nearly out of options, so if you have a better idea, I'd really like to know what it is. When Steve is on a mission, people start getting hurt. Like friends and loved ones," Janssen reminded his fellow Marine, nodding his head back toward the music and laughter coming from the parlor.

"I'm supposed to be here to protect them, but my presence here is potentially putting them in more danger," Spencer gritted his teeth at the thought of leaving the people who had become closer than family.

"You gotta do what you gotta do, man," Janssen said quietly.

"I'm just not sure what that is yet."

***

The party didn't last too long into the night, since Echo was in a delicate condition and everyone had to work the next day, but a good time was had by all. Chas received a phone call that he left the room to answer, just as they all heard a loud KABOOM! from the street in front of the inn. The guests all rushed through the foyer and out onto the porch, seeing a huge fire in the street.

"Oh my goodness, what happened?" Missy exclaimed, horrified.

"That was the catering truck," Spencer muttered, his voice thick.

Chas ran out to the porch, having just hung up the phone, glanced at the fire blazing in front of him, then grabbed Spencer by the arm.

"Did anyone call 911?" the detective asked.

"The moment I heard it," Maggie nodded.

"Good. Spence, come with me, let's see what we can do to help."

Spencer, Chas, and Kel sprinted toward the burning truck, but couldn't get close enough to see anything before heat seared their skin and smoke filled their lungs. Coughing, they retreated.

"With a fire that big and that hot, no one who was in that truck survived," Kel commented, stunned.

Spencer stared at the blaze, his throat working. He just couldn't believe that his friend was gone.

"Spencer, I need to talk with you about something," Chas said urgently, turning the Marine away from the fire and guiding him to a corner of the yard where they could talk.

"What's up?" Despite mourning his friend, the Marine was instantly clued in to the pained look in Chas's eyes.

"I just got a phone call from the lab. The finger that was delivered to the bookstore… it wasn't Jeanette Hammond's," the detective began.

The Marine stared at him, still reeling from the impact of having seen the truck, with Janssen inside it, turn into an inferno. There was a howl of sirens in the distance, adding to the gruesome, surreal atmosphere outside the inn, and Chas gazed at his friend, with compassion.

"The finger... was, is, Izzy's," he said quietly, placing a hand on Spencer's arm for support.

The young veteran's eyes narrowed, and he was instantly fully alert. "What?" he asked quietly.

"The DNA matched, Spence, I'm sorry."

"That finger showed up nearly two weeks ago," the Marine calculated. "Where is she? Have you talked to her?" he clutched at Chas's shirtfront.

The detective put a reassuring hand on top of Spencer's and the Marine let go.

"Haven't you heard from her recently? I thought you two were close?"

"No, we broke up just before the box came to Echo's store with the finger in it. I thought that I hadn't heard from her because she never wanted to speak to me again. I never imagined that something had happened to her," he shook his head, filled to the brim with regret.

"Do you have any idea why she might be a target?" Chas probed.

Spencer looked him directly in the eyes and the detective knew.

"This is because someone is after you, isn't it?"

Spencer nodded, unable, for the moment, to speak.

"I swear to you, Chas, if they hurt her..." his fists closed and he clamped his jaw shut in fury.

"Do you know who did this?"

"I think so," was the husky reply.

"And you're not going to tell me, are you, son?" Chas looked at the young man ruefully.

"No sir. You're just going to have to trust me on this one," was the determined reply.

"I have to open an investigation."

"I understand, and I'm not worried. The police will never crack this one. No offense."

"None taken. Are you going to be able to pull this off, Spence?"

"Either that or die trying," the Marine uttered, loosening his tie.

"I was afraid you'd say that," Chas looked him in the eye. "Will we see you again?" he asked, knowing what the outcome of the Marine's determination might well be.

"I certainly hope so, sir," Spencer's gaze was steady.

Impulsively, Chas pulled the younger man into a bear hug, clapping him on the back.

203

"Stay alive, Marine," he muttered, swiping covertly at his eyes.

"I'll try my best, sir," Spencer replied, and in the dark of night, he was gone.

***

Missy cried for days, lamenting the fact that Spencer hadn't been able to tell her goodbye, and that he might never return, but Chas had explained that he'd gone to find Izzy and that she should say nothing about it to anyone. She found herself glancing out the window from time to time, hoping for a glimpse of the handsome young man, whom she considered a son, and she texted him daily to let him know that she loved him and missed him, even though she knew she wouldn't receive a response. She and Echo had several good cries together, and both were trying the best they knew how to deal with such a tremendous loss.

Knowing that life must go on, and knowing that Spencer would want her to carry on, Missy went back to planning for Grayson and Sarah's upcoming wedding, sad that such a happy occasion would be overshadowed by silent pain.

Chalmers, the overseer of the vast Beckett estate and fortune, sent Patrick "Paddy" Wellsley, a flame-haired Irishman, to watch over Missy and Chas in Spencer's absence, but even the influential overseer had no idea where the Marine had gone, nor if he was okay. Paddy was a polite, hard-working respectful young man, who was ostensibly as skilled as Spencer in providing support and security, but he'd never fill the gaping hole in their hearts.

CHAPTER TWENTY
(Two weeks before)

Stumbling through unfamiliar territory, and feeling much like a character in one of her own books, Izzy Gilmore resigned herself to the fact that she was most likely going to die, and soon. Given the screaming agony in her hand that pulsed through her in nauseating waves, she felt that death, at this point, was a pretty preferable option, despite her strong will to live. She woken up in some sort of holding cell, and had found herself face to face with the evil golfer who had drugged her and kidnapped her from her home. He assured her that she would come to no harm, and that he was just waiting for the proper time to release her, but gave her no idea as to what "the proper time" might mean. Two days? Two months? Fourteen years?

Left on her own to contemplate a future consisting of sitting on a bunk in a cement cell with nothing to look forward to, aside from the delivery of a packet of military rations three times a day, Izzy began to notice things. One of the things that she noticed was that she couldn't possibly be in Florida anymore. There was a grate at the top of the high-ceilinged cell, which had fresh air flowing through it, and when the air did waft down to her, it was cool and moist, smelling of unfamiliar plants.

The resourceful author also happened to notice that the guard who brought her the food packets seemed to come at the same times every day. She didn't have a watch that told her that, she'd merely observed the position of the sun coming through the grate in her cell. The routine for the guard was exactly the same every time.

"Chow," he would announce tonelessly. Then he would touch a series of buttons on the outside of the cell door and insert a large key, turning it to the left. He would come in, set the packet, which included a napkin, plastic utensils, and condiments, down on a metal table which was bolted to the floor, and leave again. Three times a day, every day, he went through this routine. When Izzy tried to speak with him, he ignored her. If she tried to touch him, he stepped to the side to avoid her and continued on with his task. One morning he came in while she was sobbing, head between her knees and he didn't even glance in her direction.

Her bathroom was a toilet in the corner, with only a steel partition for privacy, so she made certain to use it only when she knew that a meal was not imminent, and her means of bathing was a small sink in the cement room, a rough grey washcloth and towel, and a small bar of generic soap. She used the soap to make marks on the dark grey wall of the cell next to the sink, in order to count the days, and the more marks she made, the more determined she became to escape.

Day after day of watching the guard go in and out, in and out, gave Izzy an idea, and, pretending to not be interested at all in the guard, she watched him like a hawk. She watched every movement of his hands when he operated the lock on the gate, and she learned the code, which apparently never changed, by watching the way that he moved his hand and fingers to operate the keypad.

Up center, up center, down middle, far right down, far left down... 2, 2, 5, 9, 7. Once she had the code figured out, she watched him again and again, until the series of five numbers became a chant for her that she repeated over and over, waiting for the moment that the five digits would set her free.

Steve came in to check on her one morning, when she could feel tiny droplets of rain spattering against the grate and falling into the cell, the smell of fresh rainfall filling her senses.

"I'm going away for a bit, but don't worry, young lady, you'll be fine. I'm sure that our little dilemma will be resolved soon enough," he said cheerily. "I might even bring you some ice cream if you're a good little captive while I'm gone," he teased, sounding menacingly like an unloved uncle, speaking to his ten-year-old niece.

Izzy glared at him sullenly, not speaking, but inside, her heart leapt. If Steve was leaving, that was one less person to run from when she escaped. If he was leaving today, she'd wait until tomorrow morning just to be safe, and put the plan that she'd been formulating for days into action.

"Bye now," he gave her a jaunty wave, and the door to the cell clanged shut behind him.

She got through the day by going over and over in her mind what she had to do for her freedom. Morning came early after a nearly sleepless night on the hard, thin cotton mattress that she'd been given, and she waited impatiently for her automaton guard to bring her breakfast. She'd stashed the food from lunch and dinner the day before under the mattress so that the guard wouldn't see the small, individually wrapped packets of food. She planned to take them with her when she left, soon after he dropped off her breakfast. She waited until the expressionless young man had gone, then she hurriedly forced down the packets of breakfast food that he had brought, washing it down with stale coffee and a container of juice. Tucking the remnants away into the pillowcase that she'd stripped from the pillow, along with the lunch and dinner items that she'd hidden, she sprang into action.

Izzy rolled the stiff plastic which had contained her reconstituted scrambled eggs into a tube to use as a makeshift key, bringing along the snapped-off handles of her plastic flatware for good measure.

She tied the ends of the pillowcase with her food supply in it onto one of the belt loops of her jeans so that her hands would be free, and went to work on the lock. Reaching her hand out between the bars, she punched in the code that she'd seen the guard use over and over again, 2-2-5-9-7, relieved to hear the tone which indicated that the lock was ready to open, and shoved the rolled-up plastic into the lock, wiggling it. The plastic was too soft and didn't even come close to budging the lock, so she tried again, with the two utensil handles, holding them in the keyhole and wiggling them to try to pop the lock. She pushed a bit too hard, and both handles snapped, unable to take the pressure.

Izzy ground her teeth in frustration, biting back a primal scream of angst that teased at the back of her throat. She cleaned up the shards of plastic, picking some of them out of the stubborn lock, then paced and stared, thinking. She looked all around the room for possibilities that might open the door. There were no loose screws, everything was soldered and secured to the floor, and she was at her wit's end, knowing that she was so close, with just one click of the lock keeping her from freedom. She felt the hole that the guard put the key into every day and found that it was a much larger diameter than she had expected. In fact, it was about the size of her pinky finger.

Not anxious to stick her smallest finger inside the metal tube that would eventually lead to her freedom, Izzy convinced herself that she was being a big baby, and despite the fact that it probably wouldn't work, she'd try sticking her finger in the hole to manipulate the lock. Any injury that might result would surely be better than being locked up like an animal in a cage. She pressed the code again, and this time, when she heard the mechanism get ready, she poked the pinky finger of her left hand into the hole, feeling around, and finding a metal flap that had to be the locking mechanism.

Straining her whole body, she pushed her pinky with all her might, sweat beading on her forehead, and felt it begin to give. She pushed harder, and harder, and finally with a dull thud as the lock snapped open, its metal parts gripping her finger in a most painful way, the door swung open. Elated, Izzy looked both ways down the hallway and stepped out of the cell, her finger still stuck in the lock. When she was free of the cell, she tried pulling her pinky out, but it was held fast by solid metal. She tugged and tugged, whimpering with the effort, to no avail. Finally, desperate, she assumed that if she swung the door shut, the locking mechanism would fall back into place, away from her finger, so, having no other choice, she shut the door quickly, and was totally unprepared for what came next.

A searing pain unlike anything she'd ever felt before screamed through her hand, up her arm, and into her shoulder. Her hand fell away from the door as the locking mechanism cleanly sheared off the tip of her finger. The pain took her breath away, and the room swam as she held her throbbing hand protectively against her stomach, stumbling away from the cell. She vowed to deal with the hand later, and trying desperately not to faint or throw up, she stumbled down the hallway, in the opposite direction from the one that the guard and Steve normally took.

Blindly she ran through corridor after corridor, finally finding a stairwell leading up and into the light. Two floors away, there was a door at the top of the stairwell, with a small square window near the top. Peeking through the square, Izzy saw that the building she'd been held in was surrounded by a thick forest. If she could make it to the tree line without being seen, she might have a chance at surviving. Ignoring the searing pain in her hand, she pushed against the bar to open the door, hoping that it wasn't setting off any alarms. When she didn't hear any wails of alarms or stomps of rushing feet, she took off for the trees as fast as her wobbly legs would carry her.

When Izzy got into the forest, she continued to run as though being pursued by all the hounds of hell. Her pillowcase of provisions bounced against her leg, and her left arm was tucked snugly against her stomach to protect her throbbing hand. She ran and ran and ran, until she could run no more, then she collapsed to the ground, her back against a tree, keening in pain, her sobs interrupted by bouts of dry heaving.

"Why?" she moaned, rocking to and fro, overcome with fear and pain. "Why?"

When her sobs eventually subsided, the pain in her hand practically driving her mad, she saw that the front of her t-shirt, where she'd been holding her injured hand, was soaked with blood. Knowing that she couldn't afford to pass out from blood loss, she untied her provisions bag with her right hand, and bit through the thin fabric of the pillowcase by gnawing on it like a rat. Once she'd made a hole in the loosely woven cotton, she ripped a strip away from the pillowcase with her teeth, which made her jaw and head hurt; but that kind of pain was nothing compared to what remained of her finger.

Wincing and whimpering, she wrapped her wounded finger tightly in the cloth, the pressure relieving some of the pain, and tied it snugly to the rest of her hand, using her right hand and her teeth. Once the finger was wrapped and immobilized, the pain was far more bearable, but she knew that she wouldn't last long without treatment, so Izzy planned to find a water source, attempt to eat something after she was hydrated, and continue walking until she either found help or died. Either option would suit her equally well at the moment.

***

The sun beat down on the famous author as she moved through the forest, finding neither water nor refuge. The humidity caused her clothing to stick to her in damp folds and her hair to cling to her forehead and cheeks. She was often dizzy, and had to stop more frequently than she liked, in order to rest. Her tongue felt swollen in her mouth, and her throat burned with a painful thirst. Trudging onward, she had no idea whether she'd live or die, and at this point, she couldn't really care.

One of the military food packets that she'd brought with her contained a plastic envelope of mixed fruit, and she opened it with her teeth, drinking the juice greedily. Her stomach rolled, wanting to reject the sustenance, but she willed the juice to stay down and rested. She dozed off, for how long she didn't know, but the sun was significantly lower in the sky when she awoke. Ants had gotten into her packet of fruit, but her body craved nourishment so badly that she didn't even care, and she emptied the envelope into her mouth, ants and all, chewing mechanically and swallowing because she knew that she had to.

Izzy got to her feet slowly, knowing that she had to make the most of what daylight she had, and she stood swaying for a moment, with black stars dancing in front of her eyes. Once her vision had cleared, she used every bit of her strength to keep putting one foot in front of the other. She walked until she could walk no more, then, shivering with weakness and cold, she curled up at the base of a tree, and lay down her head, not knowing if she'd ever see daylight again.

CHAPTER TWENTY-ONE
(Present)

Spencer Bengal parked his motorcycle at the end of the dirt road. He'd have to walk the rest of the way, and while right now it seemed that there was no point, he had to go to the cabin at least one last time.

When the Marine had discovered that his brother at arms, Janssen, had been living off the land in the Florida swamp, he'd found a meeting place that worked for both of them, in case one needed the other's help. The cabin was an abandoned, rough-hewn little place literally in the middle of nowhere. The closest dirt road ended a couple miles away from it, and the route from the dirt road to the cabin's humble front porch took Spencer through some rugged swamp terrain, where he not only had to watch out for cypress knees and sinkholes, but also for cottonmouths, gators, and other lethal swamp creatures.

He'd watched his friend and fellow veteran go up like a firework in the catering van, an incident which police had determined was caused by arson, and he knew that there was no point in visiting the cabin again, but he carried a six-pack of Janssen's favorite beer under his arm and trudged through two miles of treacherous Florida swamp anyway, just to get some sense of closure and honor his fallen friend.

He walked up onto the porch, the way he always had, and sat with his back up against the rough siding next to the front door, the way he always did. He cracked open one of the bottles of beer and took a good long swig, remembering what it had been like to know that no matter how bad things got, he could always come here and find Janssen, for backup, for perspective... for companionship. The two warriors understood each other, because they'd been through war and worse together, and now he was gone. The crossbow-toting, toothpick-chewing, wild man of the swamp, who'd been his friend... was gone.

Spencer took another long slug of beer and leaned his head back against the cabin, closing his eyes, lost in memories and regret.

"You plan on drinking that whole six-pack by yourself?" a familiar voice drawled. For a moment, Spencer thought that he had fallen asleep and was dreaming, but when he opened his eyes, he saw Janssen standing there, perfectly healthy, eyeballing the six-pack.

Unable to utter a sound, Spencer just stared at the scarred veteran, his heart thumping.

"You ain't even gonna talk to me, man? That's just rude, so I'm taking one," the Marine grinned, bending down to pluck a beer from its cardboard container.

He settled himself down against the siding on the other side of the door, just like old times, and drank his beer in silence.

"How the heck did you pull that off?" Spencer asked, polishing off his bottle.

"Who do you think set the fire?" Janssen chuckled. "You haven't talked to the detective yet, have you?"

"No, why?"

"They're all baffled because the truck blew up, and they didn't find any bodies."

"You staged your own death… why?"

"Because Steve Arnold knew that I was going to find you and warn you, and I want him to think that I'm dead."

"Why?"

"So you and me can go find that pretty little girlfriend of yours and finally put Steve out of his misery," Janssen shrugged.

"You know I don't operate that way," Spencer warned. "And she's not my girlfriend."

"It was just a figure of speech, I'm not going to eliminate Steve Arnold, at least I don't plan on it just yet, and it don't matter if you don't call her your girlfriend or not, you still think of her that way. Tell me I'm wrong," he challenged.

"Whatever," the Marine muttered, knowing his all-too-perceptive fellow veteran was entirely correct. "How are we going to find Steve, and how did you know that Izzy was missing?"

"We're going to start by figuring out all the possible places that he might be hiding her. Chances are, where she is, he'll be close by. How did I know she was missing? You know, same old, same old… I hear things."

"Are we leaving tonight?"

"No sense in that. We got a six-pack of beer, I've got a cooler full of venison jerky, and there are two perfectly acceptable cots inside. We'll drink up, get rested up, and hit the road early in the morning."

"Janssen?"

"Yeah?"

"I'm glad you're not dead."

"Me too, bro. Me too," the Marine opened another beer and a ghost of a smile played about his lips.

***

"The way I see it, there's only one place that makes sense for him to take her to. It's remote, it's accessible by float plane, and he could stay up there for as long as it takes without ever having to leave if he didn't want to."

"Idaho?"

"Idaho."

"That's a heck of a long way from here," Spencer sighed.

Janssen shrugged. "Meh, I know a guy who can get us there pretty quick."

"All the way there?"

"Be serious. He can get us to the lake, then we can hike in the rest of the way, unless you'd prefer to announce to Steve that we've arrived by float plane to rescue your girlfriend."

"She's not my girlfriend."

"Uh-huh. You said that."

***

Spencer adjusted the pack on his back and stretched, taking the cool mountain air into his lungs.

"It's been a while," he commented, surveying the stunning scenery around the lake.

"Not long enough," Janssen muttered, recalling a less than idyllic time that he'd spent in the beautiful locale.

"Well, the goal is to get in, grab Izzy and get out, so we won't be here that long."

"What about Steve?" Janssen raised an eyebrow.

"What *about* Steve?" Spencer challenged, his jaw set.

"If we don't do something about him, one way or another, he's just going to continue, and clearly he's not afraid to escalate," the scarred veteran pointed out.

"We'll cross that bridge when we come to it."

With a grunt and a sigh, Janssen started making his way through the woods, toward the dark ops compound hidden deep in the primitive area.

CHAPTER TWENTY-TWO
(Present)

Izzy opened her eyes slowly, blinking in the bright light. She was startled to find that she was lying on a rough cotton quilt, and the smell of frying meat surrounded her.

"Mornin," a gruff voice greeted her.

There was a grey-haired, heavily bearded man standing at the stove, in what looked like a small hunting lodge, tending the meat that she smelled. Izzy blinked at the man, confused, scared, and hungry.

"Where am I?" she whispered, her throat dry.

"Middle o' nowhere," the mountain man in the worn plaid shirt and faded jeans grunted. "Want some coffee?"

"Yes, please," she sat up, finding herself dressed in an oversized thermal shirt that came halfway to her knees. She drew the wool blanket that she'd been lying under around her protectively.

"Don't worry none, little girl. I ain't got no intentions on ya," the man said, handing her a steaming cup of coffee that smelled like heaven. Her stomach growled.

"Sip on that, and if you keep it down, you can try a bit of venison sausage," he gestured to the sizzling pan on the stove.

"I'm Izzy," she said tentatively, taking a small sip of the strong brew and loving it. The hot dark liquid felt glorious in her parched throat.

"Norm," he nodded at her introduction. Clearly he was a man of few words.

"How did I get here, Norm?" she asked, not certain if she wanted to hear his answer.

"Found ya in the woods, out cold. Thought you were dead at first. You were pretty close. Lost a lotta blood," he recounted, flipping the sausage patties, which landed with a hiss on the skillet.

"How long have I been here?"

"Bout two weeks," he shrugged.

"Two weeks?" she was astonished.

"Yep, you were feverish and delirious, slippin' in and out of the real world for quite a while. I used some Native remedies on ya, and some pain relievers, burnt the infection out, and hoped for the best."

"Burnt the…" Izzy swallowed, turning a light shade of greenish grey.

"Your hand, little girl," he pointed at her left hand and she looked down. Seeing the homemade bandages on what was left of her pinky finger, she was suddenly assaulted by memories of what had happened, and her head swam a bit.

"Easy now, hold steady girl, you'll be all right," Norm watched her from his spot at the stove.

Izzy shivered and swallowed, determined not to fall apart.

"Thank you… for helping me," she said, suddenly embarrassed when she realized the potential extent of the things that this grizzled old man must've had to do for her over the course of the last two weeks.

"You were wounded. Couldn't just leave ya to die, wouldn't be right," he replied, staring intently at the pan in front of him. "Think you can eat?"

Izzy's stomach growled in response and she nodded.

"Lemme git ya over to the table and you can give it a try," Norm directed, reaching for her good hand.

She slowly rose to her feet, her head throbbing slightly, her knees weak and threatening to buckle. Norm put his hand at the small of her back to steady her while still holding her right hand. He smelled of wood smoke and sausage, and she found that somehow comforting. They made their way to the crude, hand-hewn table and chairs and she sat, exhausted from the small effort. Norm put a plate in front of her and she saw that he'd used his spatula to mince the sausage patty into tiny pieces.

"Hope ya ain't a leftie," he said, handing her a fork.

"I'm not," Izzy replied, spearing a tiny piece of sausage and putting it in her mouth.

It may have been just because of extreme hunger, but the morsel of food was the best sausage she'd ever tasted, and she chewed slowly, savoring the crunchy spicy goodness of it.

"That's it," Norm nodded. "Take it slow so you don't sick it back up."

"Have I been… sick since I've been here?"

"More than once. It happens. I had to feed you broth cuz you weren't conscious enough to eat real food."

"I could've died," Izzy murmured. "You saved my life."

"I thought you were gonna," he nodded. "Takin' care of ya was easier than buryin' ya woulda been," he cracked a smile.

Izzy smiled back.

"Where are we?" she asked for the second time.

"Idaho. Part of the state called the primitive area. No cars allowed."

She stared at him.

"Idaho?"

"Yep."

"I've never heard of a primitive area."

"That's kinda the point," he blinked at her.

"Oh. Well... how do I get out of here?"

"Condition yer in? Ya don't. At least not 'til yer healthy enough to hike a fair distance."

"How did I get here in the first place?"

"After I found ya, I made a stretcher outta some limbs and rope and dragged ya here. Took me a coupla days."

"I owe you my life, thank you," Izzy bit her lip.

"No thanks needed. Just work on gettin' better and stronger so we can get ya outta here before the snow flies," he advised, shoveling bites of sausage into his mouth.

"I will," she promised, taking another bite and washing it down with coffee. "Where are my clothes?"

"Yonder," Norm pointed with his fork to a neatly folded pile sitting on a shelf over the bed. "You'll want to get cleaned up, I imagine, so I'll heat up some shower water after breakfast."

"Thank you. Thank you so much… for everything," Izzy felt tears spring to her eyes.

"Ain't nothin," he replied gruffly, taking his empty plate to the small sink and rinsing it. "You'll have some hot water in about half an hour."

CHAPTER TWENTY-THREE

Spencer and Janssen stood behind the cover of trees and shrubs at the edge of the tree line which bordered the compound. The sight of the squat grey building provoked negative reactions in both of them, and the thought that Izzy was within its walls filled Spencer with a powerful rage that he had to stifle in order to think straight.

"Hey, check this out," Janssen was staring down at a particular spot on a leafy bush.

"What?" Spencer whispered, moving closer. He looked down and saw what Janssen had discovered. "Blood trail," he commented, his stomach dropping.

"Yup. If we get in there and she's not there, we'll at least know where to pick up her trail. She's one spunky little character if she gave Steve and his boys the slip."

"Yeah, she's tough, but she's also bleeding."

"You gotta focus, man. We've got no way of knowing that she's the one who's bleeding. Steve's guys could've snagged a rabbit for all we know," Janssen said in a low voice.

Spencer gave him a look. They both knew that the likelihood of the blood trail being from Izzy was more probable.

"Let's wait until dark to get inside. Steve probably isn't even here if Izzy escaped, and his guys will almost certainly be asleep."

From having spent time at the facility in the past, the Marines knew the coverage area of the security cameras, and planned a route to get inside without being followed by electronic eyes. They knew where the security staff worked and slept, and they knew where Steve's private quarters were located. The plan was to incapacitate the security staff first and then descend upon Steve Arnold's room before he knew what was happening, if he was even on the premises at all.

To kill time until nightfall, Spencer and Janssen followed the blood trail into the woods, getting a sense of the direction that Izzy had taken.

"Looking at the spatter patterns that she left, it looks like she was moving pretty fast," Janssen observed.

"She runs every morning, so she's in good shape."

"That'll help her odds of survival."

They came to the base of a tree where the blood was pooled a bit, and noted that several saplings had been hacked down nearby, and there were drag marks on the forest floor, leading away from the tree and ending the blood trail.

"Well, unless your girl made a stretcher out of saplings and dragged it behind her, somebody's got her," Janssen mused.

"Let's hope it's someone with good intentions," Spencer's jaw flexed. "Let's get back to the compound to make sure she's not there, and as soon as we've taken care of the guards and Steve, we'll follow the drag marks and find her."

"You got it," Janssen nodded, heading back toward the tree line at a fast clip, Spencer on his heels.

***

Steve Arnold was livid. Izzy Gilmore had been his bargaining chip, the one thing that would force Spencer Bengal into accepting his assignment, which would earn Steve some much-needed brownie points with Command.

"You had one job," he raged, after packaging Izzy's finger up and sending it off to Echo's store, in the hands of a trusted employee, to make certain that it would get Spencer's attention. "All you had to do was feed her and keep her here until my operative arrived. How hard is that? And yet you managed to screw it up," he screamed in the guard's face, spittle flying.

Steve very rarely lost his cool, and when he did, people had a habit of disappearing or dying, so the guard should have been trembling in his boots, yet he wasn't.

"Are you listening to me?" he raged on, red-faced, a vein on his forehead pulsing.

"No," the guard replied mildly. "I'm done listening to you."

Before Steve could react, he felt hard, cold steel against his temple and sensed, rather than heard, a finger squeezing the trigger of a handgun, millimeters from his grey matter. Another twitch and the gun would fire. Rather than replying immediately, his fury turned swiftly to cold calculation and he assessed his situation. Because his captive had been a small female, he'd only left one operative in charge of her care. Now, with the unknown gunman, there were at least two operatives on site. He was outnumbered, but he doubted seriously that he was outsmarted.

"What do you want?" he asked coolly, every last trace of authoritarian hostility absent from his voice.

"We want out," the guard in front of him said, simply. "We're done taking orders, putting our lives on the line for causes we don't believe in, and never having anything close to what resembles a normal life. We've more than covered our tours of duty and we want out. New identities and a new start, non-negotiable, and we're not going to release you until you make it happen."

"Command will never go for it. It's out of my hands," Steve replied reasonably.

"They will if you convince them that the program isn't effective, that you've failed, that they need to take a new direction."

"If I say anything remotely like that, they're going to know that it's under duress," he snickered.

Steve had a point, everyone who knew him knew that he had supreme self-confidence which often crossed the line into arrogance. Admitting defeat was not within his emotional framework. The gunman behind him finally spoke.

"If you don't convince them, the only thing left of you will be a fine pink mist," he growled. "We'll be out of here under a new name long before Command even realizes you're missing. Either way, we win. You get to choose whether we win and you live, or we win and you die. I'm happy either way."

"Smitty... I should have known," he remarked, recognizing the gunman's voice. "You really think you're going to get away with this?"

"One way or another, yes. Absolutely, we're going to get away with this," the eyes of the guard in front of him were like chips of flint.

Steve studied him for a long moment and knew that he had to buy himself some time to think.

"I'll need some time to come up with what I'm going to say to Command, as well as an alternate plan that I can propose to take the place of the black ops program. They would expect nothing less, and I have to sound legit if this is going to work. Give me forty-eight hours."

"You have twenty-four, and you're going to spend it in solitary, with no means of communication."

They made Steve strip down to his skivvies and searched him for any weapons or communication devices. Finding none, they put him in the cell from which he'd extracted Izzy's finger. There was dried blood on the lock, the bars, and the floor that no one had bothered to clean up. He couldn't imagine the disorganized mess that black ops would become without his leadership. He knew that he had to figure out a way to neutralize these two hostile operatives, and wished that he'd known what he would be walking into when he came back.

***

Wearing night vision goggles, Spencer and Janssen made their way toward the compound. They'd been observing it for several hours and had seen no one come in or out. Their best guess was that one or two operatives would be on site, and perhaps Steve Arnold as well. Whether or not Steve would care enough about Izzy to send a search team out to look for her, assuming that she actually had escaped, was anyone's guess.

The duo moved quickly toward their objective, hoping that the alarm code for entrances hadn't changed. Janssen scanned the area around the door, not seeing any new hookups indicating that it was actively armed for security, he opened the door. Izzy had just happened to find the one route to safety that would allow her to exit in secrecy.

They moved silently into the stairwell, heading downstairs toward the crew area. Slipping along the walls like mere shadows, they took off their goggles when they approached the area where any active operatives should be. The halls were lit here, and the cameras were fully functional, so they had to move fast and hope to surprise any on-site personnel before they noticed their presence.

Janssen peered into the lounge area of the crew station and saw two operatives sitting on a couch, with their backs to the door. He looked over his shoulder at Spencer, held up two fingers and pointed at the door. Spencer nodded briefly, and signaled Janssen to move forward. Bursting through the door, the Marines surprised Smitty and the guard, incapacitating them with choke holds before they knew what hit them. With his ever-present roll of duct tape, Janssen secured both men so that they wouldn't be a cause for concern, and he and Spencer went in search of Steve.

They found their nemesis kicked back on the cot in his cell, looking confident and content.

"Smitty brought you two in on this?" he asked, hands folded behind his head. "I underestimated him."

Spencer and Janssen exchanged a look, which Steve didn't miss.

"Wait a minute, you're not in on this, are you?" he sat up, frowning.

"You're talking gibberish, man," Janssen drawled, chewing on his ever-present toothpick.

"Get me out of here, and I'll explain," he ordered.

"I think I kind of like you in there," Spencer smirked.

"If you'd like some information about your pretty little girlfriend, you'll be getting me out of here. The more time you waste here, the more danger she's in. Up to you," Steve shrugged.

"Don't play me," Spencer shot back. "You don't have any more idea of where she is than we do."

"So you're not the one who rescued her," Steve pounced on the Marine's admission. "Good to know. Now, what are you doing in here with me, rather than out there looking for her?"

"Bargaining," Janssen replied.

"What makes you think you're in a position to bargain?" Steve snickered.

"I ain't the one in a cage, man," he shrugged.

"I'll be out of here soon enough."

"Really?" Spencer raised an eyebrow.

"It's only a matter of time before Command sends a team to find me."

"Bull," Janssen chuckled. "Command is used to you disappearing for weeks at a time. There's no time crunch for us. You give us what we want or you can stay in that hamster cage for a good long time."

"You ops idiots are all beginning to sound alike," Steve sighed. "What do you want?"

"We'll discuss it with you while we're on the road. Hang tight, we'll get you some clothes, and we'll be out of here within the hour."

"On the road?" This revelation took Steve by surprise. "We're going somewhere?"

"Yeah, buddy, we're going on a rescue op and you're going to be a good boy or we'll shoot you and leave you for the bears," Janssen said casually, turning to go.

"I'm not going anywhere with you."

"Suit yourself, but we're going to turn the heat off when we go."

***

Steve Arnold trudged along behind Janssen, knowing that if he did anything to thwart the plans of his two most dangerous operatives, Spencer would incapacitate him immediately. He'd agreed to come along after they threatened to leave him in the cell indefinitely, the look in their eyes cluing him in to the fact that they weren't bluffing.

The two Marines had memorized the path that the blood trail had taken through the woods, and they followed it, wearing night vision goggles. Steve was forced to rely on keeping Janssen in his sights, unaided by goggles. When they arrived at the spot where the saplings had been cut, Janssen had to watch the ground much more carefully in order to follow the drag path, but whoever had dragged Izzy away hadn't bothered to cover their tracks, so they made good time, arriving at Norm's cabin just before sunrise.

The halted in order to observe the small structure from a safe distance away, shielded by trees. When a gruff voice ordered them to put their hands up and turn around slowly, they were taken aback.

239

"What do you boys think you're doin' here on my property?" Norm demanded, training a loaded shotgun on the trio.

"It's actually government property," Steve drawled, impatient at being threatened by a civilian.

"No worries, old timer," Janssen replied, shooting Steve a nasty look. "We ain't here to cause no trouble. We're just looking for a friend of ours, Izzy Gilmore."

"Friend, huh?" Norm eyed them suspiciously, not lowering his weapon. "You boys the kind of friend that would cut off a ladies' finger and leave her to fend for herself in the forest?"

Spencer slowly turned his head to gaze at Steve, murderous rage coloring his vision.

"No way, man. We came to rescue her from those guys and found that she'd already escaped," Janssen answered easily.

"What guys?" the mountain man demanded.

"Military types. There's some kind of facility not too far from here. That's where she escaped from."

"How do I know that you're not the ones who hurt her?"

Janssen inclined his head toward Spencer. "Take him with you and ask her. I'll stay here with this dirtbag and wait for you."

No one in Spencer's life had ever seen Janssen in person, aside from him making an appearance as a waiter for Echo and Kel's wedding dinner, and he wanted to keep it that way. Sending Spencer in to rescue Izzy meant that he'd be left to make certain that Steve complied with their request for freedom, and he'd use whatever means necessary. Spencer often acted as a buffer, using physical violence as a last resort. Janssen was highly skilled in the application of specific force in order to obtain objectives, and Steve knew that he wouldn't hesitate to practice his craft.

Norm nodded.

"All right, but if either one of you boys try anything, pretty boy here is a dead man."

"Deal," Janssen nodded.

Spencer locked his fingers behind his head and allowed the older man to rest the barrel of his gun between his shoulder blades as they walked back to the cabin. When he got to the door, Norm told him to open it, leaving the gun firmly in place. The Marine opened the door, and his heart pounded with relief when he saw Izzy, sitting near the small wood stove in a crude rocking chair.

"Friend or foe?" Norm demanded when she looked up and stared at Spencer, wide-eyed.

She stood up, her eyes meeting Spencer's, and he had no idea how she'd answer Norm's question.

"Friend," she whispered, a lonely tear trailing down her cheek.

At last, Norm lowered his weapon, standing it in a corner of the room.

"You okay?" Spencer asked in a low voice, keeping a tight rein on the emotions that were flooding through him. Izzy was thinner, and a bit unkempt, but she was alive.

She nodded and held up her left hand, her pinky wrapped.

"I know," he said, closing his eyes briefly, his heart contracting with grief at what the missing digit might mean to the author's career. "Can you travel?"

"She's a mite weak yet," Norm interjected.

"We can move slowly if we need to. You've taken good care of her, but we need to get her to a hospital and get her checked out. I'm going to go tell the others that she's safe, then we're going to meet up with a float plane and get her out of here."

The Marine turned back to Izzy.

"I'll be right back, I promise. We're going to get you home," he said, his blue eyes earnest.

Izzy nodded again, tears flowing freely now, and Spencer left the cabin.

"Take Steve back to the compound, and do whatever you have to do to achieve the objective," Spencer directed. "Contact your buddy and let him know that we'll be at the transport spot in about four hours."

"Roger that," Janssen nodded.

"What objective?" Steve narrowed his eyes, less than pleased at the prospect of being left alone with Janssen.

Neither Marine dignified his question with a reply.

"See you on the other side, brother," Janssen stuck a fresh toothpick in between his teeth.

"Sooner, rather than later, I hope," Spencer shook his hand.

CHAPTER TWENTY-FOUR

The physician's assistant in the first town outside of the Primitive Area checked out Izzy's injured hand and nodded, impressed.

"Well, it'll still need to be evaluated by a specialist, but you've done a good job of cleaning and treating the wound. I'll set you up with some antibiotics and you should be more than okay to travel back home," he smiled professionally.

"Thank you," Izzy murmured, and slid off the exam table.

"No problem, just stop by the front desk on your way out, and the nurse will meet you there with a ten-day supply."

The PA left, leaving Izzy and Spencer alone in the exam room.

"Can I take you to the airport?" Spencer offered, his eyes filled with concern.

She shook her head.

"No, it's fine. I can get a cab," she said quietly, unable to meet his gaze, and face the naked pain in his eyes.

"I'm glad you're okay," he murmured, turning to go.

"Spence," she called out, causing him to stop in his tracks and turn slowly to face her.

"Yeah?"

"Thank you," her lower lip trembled and her eyes welled.

His shoulders slumped and he nodded. "You're welcome, Izzy."

Spencer Bengal was a stranger in a strange land. He couldn't go back to Calgon—he didn't want to put Missy and Chas in danger if Steve had anyone out looking for him, he couldn't go back to the compound, because he wasn't sure that he wanted to witness the tactics that Janssen might be using to secure their freedom, and he couldn't go back to the Beckett estate in New York, because that would be the first place that Steve's watchdogs would look for him, so, for the first time in a very long time, he was on his own. He checked his watch, and knew that Izzy would be boarding a plane back to Florida in about an hour. He'd wait until he was certain that she was gone, then he'd head to the airport, passport in hand, and choose a random destination where he could wait for word from Janssen. The swamp rat would find him... he always did.

CHAPTER TWENTY-FIVE

"I'm a terrible person, Echo, I really am," Missy shook her head.

"Oh stop it, you are not," Echo peered over the top of her tea mug at her stressed-out friend. "What would even make you say such a silly thing?"

"Well, honestly, with everything that's been happening around here lately, I just have no desire to plan Grayson and Sarah's wedding," she confessed, feeling awful about it.

"While that's entirely understandable, we don't exactly have a choice in the matter. The invitations have been sent, girl. We've got to pull this together for that young man whom we both love."

"I know, it's just so hard to get into it. I worry about Spencer all the time," Missy sighed.

"Look, I miss Spencer too, honey, but we both know—beyond a shadow of a doubt—that that boy can take care of himself. I know he'll be back some day. He didn't just walk away from here, never planning to return. We owe it to Grayson to focus our attention right now on the beginning of his new life with Sarah. We've got to support him in this."

"I know you're right, my heart just hurts," Missy admitted.

"Mine too, but the best way that we can deal with that is to make sure that Grayson and Sarah have the most amazing wedding ever."

"Okay, let's talk about logistics, then," Missy said, brushing at her eyes and getting back to business. "The inn is full, so I've given everyone on the guest list a list of nearby hotels. We can shuttle them back and forth if we need to."

"Good, when do Grayson and Sarah get in?" Echo asked, glad that her friend had switched gears before they'd both turned into blubbering messes.

"Next week. Sarah wanted to be here early enough to be involved in the decorating, and Grayson insisted upon making the cake himself. It's going to be so much fun having them around again."

"Yes, it will. Are Ben and Cheryl going to be able to make it out here for the wedding?"

"Unfortunately, no. It's too close to Cheryl's due date," Missy replied ruefully.

Ben and Cheryl had managed Missy's cupcake shops, one in LaChance, the other in the nearby town of Dellville, in Louisiana, when Grayson first started working there, and the three of them were like siblings. Grayson was terribly disappointed, but completely understanding, when he'd heard the news. Knowing how badly the couple had wanted to be involved in their "little brother's" wedding, Missy and Chas had bought plane tickets for the newlyweds so that they could fly to Mexico for their honeymoon, via California, where they'd get a chance to visit with Ben and Cheryl for a few days. The gift of the honeymoon was a surprise that would be revealed at the reception.

Missy and Echo were poring over the wedding planner book, when the chimes over the door to Cupcakes in Paradise jingled, signaling a customer, or so they thought.

"Well, if it ain't Melissa Gladstone-Beckett and her little hippie friend," Petaluma Myers's nasal voice emphasized each syllable of Missy's name. The hateful twang seemed to bounce off the walls of the cozy little shop.

"Petaluma… what a… wonderful surprise," Missy rose and went to hug Grayson's mother, holding her breath against the wave of alcoholic fumes radiating from the woman. "The wedding isn't for another week…"

"Oh, I know," she nodded, looking around the shop as though she were casing it. "I just thought that y'all might need some help with wedding stuff, so I caught a ride with a truck driver who was headin' down here and showed up early. You're welcome," she proclaimed, patting her ratty, bleached-blonde hair with grey and brown roots.

"We're pretty much finished," Echo broke in, finally finding her voice, once the shock of seeing the woman had subsided. "Maybe you could spend some time on the beach," she suggested.

"Nuh-uh, no way," she shook her head, knocking her a bit off balance. "This is my baby boy's weddin. I'm gonna check through everythin that y'all have done and make sure that there ain't nothin that got screwed up or left out," said the woman who hadn't provided food or shelter for her sensitive son for years, even when he was in school.

"Well, how kind of you," Missy said quickly, before Echo could shoot off the reply that immediately came to mind. "I'll be happy to sit down with you and show you the plans. Maybe after dinner tonight? Where are you staying?"

"Thought you owned the hotel over there," Petaluma pointed a knobby finger at the inn.

"Oh... well, yes, Chas and I do own the bed and breakfast, but we're full from now until well after the wedding is over. You didn't check into a hotel yet?"

"Nope, that good for nothin son of mine told me that I could stay with y'all," the skinny forty-something in a bubble-gum pink tank top and jean short-shorts insisted.

Grayson had called Missy weeks ago and specifically requested that if his mother should choose to attend, she was not to stay at the inn, because he didn't want her upsetting the other guests.

"Oh, I'm sure there must have been some misunderstanding. Would you like me to help you find a hotel room?" Missy offered, her stomach sinking with a premonition of doom.

"I ain't got no money for no dang hotel. Grayson should be putting me up, it's his weddin," Petaluma pursed her lips and tossed her tangled mass of hair over one shoulder.

Missy looked helplessly at Echo, who was clearly simmering at Grayson's mother's attitude.

"Let's deal with that later. Petaluma, how about we treat you to a nice dinner, and then we can talk about your accommodations later," Echo suggested, desperately trying to think of a polite way to send the woman home.

"That's right, y'all need to show me a good time, I'm a guest after all," she sniffed.

"Do you have any luggage?" Missy asked.

"Just this," Petaluma swung a dingy backpack down from her shoulder.

Missy saw the bedraggled bag and made a mental note to give the shop a thorough cleaning when Petaluma departed.

"Okay, Echo, can you go introduce Petaluma to Paddy? He can show her how to use the shower in the pool cabana so that she can freshen up and maybe have some coffee before dinner," Missy gave her friend a pointed look.

"Petaluma, you're more than welcome to borrow something from my closet to wear to dinner if you'd like," she offered. "Echo would be happy to grab a dress for you."

"Ya got anything that doesn't look like you stole it from June Cleaver? No offense, honey, but if I had a rack like you've got, I wouldn't be hidin it under those cutesy little blouses. Gotta accentuate the positive, know what I mean?" she cackled.

"I'm sure she'll find something very becoming," Missy smiled tightly.

"Becoming," she mocked. "Well I'll feel like I'm just havin lunch with the queen. Ta-ta," she waved, weaving her way out the door behind Echo.

Missy rubbed her temples and sniffed the air, deciding that she was definitely going to close the shop and clean. It was shaping up to be one heck of a pre-wedding week already.

CHAPTER TWENTY-SIX

Missy and Echo opted to have their "girl's night" with Petaluma at a seafood shack on the beach which didn't serve alcohol. Echo had found a sleeveless blue dress in Missy's closet that she thought Petaluma might like, and she rejected it after trying it on, saying that it "hung on her like a sack, and didn't showcase her assets." So, she sat slurping down a hotdog, with a side of onion rings, wearing tight white denim shorts, chewed-up flip flops, and a stained, skintight grey tank top with the words "Git Some" emblazoned in white across her "assets."

"So, Petaluma… I called every hotel in town, and everything is booked right now because it's wedding season, and there are a couple of conventions happening. Do you have any friends or family down here who could take you in?" Missy asked, halfway hoping that the woman would just give up and go back to Louisiana.

Petaluma's cheeks were stuffed full of food and she chewed with her mouth slightly open, making Missy wonder how long it had been since her last meal.

"Conventions, huh? I like conventions... lotsa guys around who can appreciate a good woman," she nodded, swallowing, then taking another huge bite of her hotdog.

Missy looked at Echo, eyes wide.

"So, where can we drop you off after dinner?" Echo asked bluntly, hoping they'd get a straight answer this time.

"Wherever," she shrugged, talking with her mouth full. "It ain't like I got someplace to go. Weather's nice, so I'll probably sleep under a bridge or somethin, no big deal."

Missy was horrified. "Oh, absolutely not, that's not safe," she exclaimed. "Echo, does Kel maybe know someone... ?"

"Seriously?" Echo blinked at her friend. Her fiancé was a pampered member of a privileged class. It was doubtful that he'd know where a drunken vagabond could safely flop for the night.

Missy pleaded with her eyes. "It's for Grayson," she mouthed, as Petaluma sucked cola loudly through her straw.

Echo sighed and rolled her eyes. "Hey Petaluma, tell you what... I have an extra room at my house. You can stay there tonight and hopefully we can find other arrangements for you tomorrow, how's that sound?"

Petaluma stuffed an onion ring, dripping with ketchup, into her mouth. When a blob of the red sauce landed on her leg, she swiped it up with her finger and sucked it off.

"Dunno," she shrugged. "Got a comfortable bed?"

Echo's mouth dropped open in astonishment, and before Missy could intervene, she blurted, "Well, I suppose it's more comfortable than sleeping under a bridge."

"Hope so," Petaluma was unfazed. "You gonna eat the rest of that?" she asked, eyeing the remains of Missy's lobster roll.

"No, feel free. Somehow, I don't have much of an appetite," Missy sighed, looking at her friend with gratitude.

***

After dinner, Petaluma tried to wheedle the girls into taking her to a local bar for a drink, but Missy claimed a headache, and Echo was pregnant, so they were able to avoid that particular activity. Missy dropped Echo off at her house, with Petaluma trailing behind her, and mouthed "Be Nice!" to her friend, who wrinkled her nose.

"Howdy neighbor," Echo heard an all-too-familiar voice call out from the house next door.

Her neighbor, Loud Steve, who was known for blasting the music in his compact pickup truck so loudly that he could be heard from blocks away, was standing on his front porch, a beer in one hand, and a can of bug spray in the other. Echo sighed inwardly, having no patience for the obnoxious man who never failed to hit on her.

"Hi Steve," she replied wearily.

"Who's that hot little thang you've got there with ya?" he asked, raising his beer and eyeing Petaluma.

"Well, ain't you sweet?" she called back with a wave.

"Why don't y'all come over here and hang out for a bit," he invited, having eyes only for Grayson's scantily clad mother. "I got beer and bug spray, and I can light us a bonfire if ya want."

"Tempting, but no, we have an early day tomorrow," Echo replied, heading up the steps to her cozy cottage.

"Says you," Petaluma shot back, making a beeline for Steve's cooler. "I'm on vacation, honey, and I sure as heck got time to have a beer with this fine-lookin man." She settled into a lawn chair that he unfolded for her, and held her arms and legs out for him to spray her down with bug repellent. Echo shuddered and pitied any bug that would venture close to those two anyway.

"Suit yourself. Guest room is down the hall, second door on the right."

"G'night," Petaluma trilled, mocking her and waving.

She looked at Steve and he looked at her and they cracked up.

***

When Echo got up the next morning, her living room smelled like a brewery, and Grayson's mother was passed out, fully clothed, on her couch, reeking of beer, smoke and bug spray. Sighing and shaking her head, Echo left the snoring woman where she was and headed out the door to the cupcake shop.

"Oh no, what's wrong?" Missy asked, when she saw her friend's face.

"Petaluma got together with Loud Steve last night for an impromptu beer party and is now sleeping it off on my couch," Echo replied, reaching for not one, not two, but three of Missy's vanilla bean vegan cupcakes.

"Oh sugar, I'm sorry. I just hated the thought of her sleeping under a bridge," Missy bit her lip.

"At this point, I'm thinking that the bridge is an excellent option," Echo muttered crossly.

"Let me go make you some herbal tea," Missy offered, watching her friend wolf down the cupcakes, barely pausing for breath.

When she returned to the front of the cupcake shop, Missy was rather surprised to see Timothy Eckels, the mortician and medical examiner, timidly entering.

"Well good morning, Mr. Eckels," Missy greeted him.

"Hey Tim," Echo chimed in.

She knew him better than Missy did, because his house was on the other side of hers. Loud Steve lived on the left and Timothy Eckels on the right.

"Uh, hello," he raised a hand in greeting, hating to have to draw from his limited reservoir of social skills. "I don't want to be a bother, but, may I talk with you for a moment, Miss Willis?" he asked Echo.

"Of course, have a seat," she patted the chair next to her. Tim was an odd duck, which Echo found utterly endearing.

"Would you like a cupcake and some coffee, Mr. Eckels?" Missy asked.

Tim blinked at her for a moment. "Yes, of course I would," he nodded, peering at her as though she'd be silly to think otherwise.

"Coming right up," she replied cheerily.

She'd encountered Tim on several occasions before, and liked him, despite his social incompetence. He was straightforward, honest, and smart, and Missy sort of felt sorry for him.

"So what's up?" Echo paused in between bites to ask, taking a sip of her tea.

He straightened his already rigid frame and assumed a beleaguered look. "What is up is that your insufferable neighbor and his equally appalling girlfriend verbally assaulted me when I left my home this morning, throwing threw beer cans at my head," he regarded her soberly, his eyes huge behind his coke-bottle lenses. "The woman said that she was your friend, but I didn't believe her for an instant, and then… she went in your house," he confided, clearly gravely concerned. "I felt that I had to come find you and let you know."

Echo sighed and Missy set a luscious Pink Lemonade cupcake in front of Tim, along with a mug of coffee, a pitcher of cream, and a pot of sugar cubes. The mortician meticulously attended to his coffee, then carefully peeled the wrapper away from his cupcake, breaking the bottom of the cake off and placing it gingerly on top of the frosting so that he could take bites without getting his hands and face messy.

"I'm sorry about that, Tim. I'll talk to her."

"Then she IS your friend?" He blinked rapidly, astonished.

"No. That is not even close to how I would describe our relationship," Echo sighed again. "But she does happen to be staying with me temporarily."

"Oh dear. Well, you might have to think about cleaning your carpets, I heard some awful retching noises after she dashed inside," he confided, taking a bite of cupcake.

"Great. Just great," she dropped her head into her hands.

"Oh honey, I'm so sorry," Missy's hands covered her throat in horror. "I'm gonna call the carpet cleaners right now and tell them I'll pay them extra," she promised, dashing from the room and pulling out her phone.

She came back a few minutes later, and Tim had gone, leaving a ten-dollar bill to cover his coffee, cupcake, and tip.

"Oh, he didn't have to do that. I wouldn't have charged him anything," Missy commented, stuffing the bill in the tip jar.

"He insisted," Echo replied. "Tim's a good guy. A little misunderstood, but definitely good."

"It sure seems that way," Missy agreed.

Her phone rang and she pulled it out of her pocket, delighted when she saw who was calling.

"Grayson, sweetie, how are you?"

Echo watched Missy's face changed from delighted to concerned, to frightened, in rapid succession. She caught snippets of Missy's side of the conversation when she came back to the table after refilling her tea.

"Are you sure? And there's been no word? Oh, I'm so sorry honey. Yes, keep me posted. Okay... Bye."

Missy hung up the phone, looking stunned.

"What is it?" Echo demanded, putting down her tea cup.

"That was Grayson... there may not be a wedding... Sarah is missing."

Made in the USA
Lexington, KY
21 December 2017

X